Trailing Fireflies

SAURABH JADHAV

This is a work of fiction. Names, characters, businesses, places, events and incidents are either products of the author's imagination or used in a fictitious manner. Any resemblance to actual persons, living or dead, or actual events is purely coincidental.

First Edition: November 2025
Printed in India

Printed at: Gapmeta Ventures Pvt.Ltd, Navi Mumbai
Typeset in Garamond

ISBN: 978-93-6070-837-5

Cover Design: Prajakta Sawant

STORYMIRROR
Stories that reflect you

Publisher: StoryMirror Infotech Pvt. Ltd.
Unit No-F/705, 7th Floor, Kailas Corporate Lounge,
Veer Savarkar Road, Vikhroli Park Site,
Vikhroli West, Mumbai-400079,
Maharashtra, India.

Web: storymirror.com
Facebook: @storymirror
Twitter: @story_mirror
Instagram: @storymirror
Email: marketing@storymirror.com

TABLE OF CONTENTS

DEDICATION

To my parents, for their endless love, patience, and sacrifices.
To my Wife, who gave a new meaning to my life.
To my friends, who never let me forget who I was.
To my extended family, who stood beside me when I faltered.
To every dreamer who ever feared falling—may you always rise again.
And for the reader—may you find pieces of your own story hidden in mine.

ACKNOWLEDGEMENT

WRITING THIS book has been a journey of years, filled with hesitation, self-doubt, and hope. I want to thank my family for their unwavering support.

My wife, thank you for your patience, your love, and for holding me together when I doubted myself. This book could not exist without you.

My brothers Rohit, Sudarshan, Aniket, Nishant, Nikhil and Dikshant for always being my pillars.

And the members of my family, whose words and encouragement kept me going.

My friends from my cricket days, especially Rahul and Mayur.

To the readers who choose to pick up this story—thank you for giving Aditya and Radhika a space in your heart.

PREFACE

THERE ARE moments in life that arrive like fireflies in the dark—brief, delicate, and unforgettable. They shimmer only for a heartbeat, yet their glow lingers, guiding us through the shadows long after they have disappeared.

This story is born from such moments. Trailing Fireflies is not about triumphs or certainties, but about fragility—of love, of memory, of the human spirit when tested by time and loss. It is about Aditya, but it is also about all of us—about the pieces we lose along the way, and the quiet strength we discover in learning to live with what remains.

As you turn these pages, may you find a reflection of your own journey—the laughter that once echoed, the silences that still ache, and the courage that flickers even in the darkest of nights.

For in the end, we are all chasing fireflies: fleeting lights that remind us that even the smallest glow is enough to keep us moving forward.

CHAPTER I
THE DREAM & THE FALL

A BIKE SKIDDED across the bridge, crashing violently against the railing before vanishing into the abyss below with its rider. The thick fog swallowed everything in seconds. My brain froze. For a moment, it felt as if the ground beneath me had slipped away. My heart pounded like war drums in my chest. I wanted to run, to scream, to do something, but my legs were heavy, as though chained to the road. Somehow, I forced myself forward, stumbling to the edge. Leaning over the guardrail, I squinted into the void. All I saw was a restless sea of white mist, endless. No trace of the rider. No clue of what lay hidden below.

"Help!" My voice tore through the silence, echoing back to me like a cruel reminder that no one was around. The bridge stretched empty on both sides, hauntingly still. Panic gripped me. Time was slipping away. I had to act.

With a surge of reckless resolve, I climbed onto the railing. For one last breath, I hesitated—then leapt into the mist. The clouds swallowed me whole. My body kept falling… falling… endlessly falling into the unknown.

It was already nine. The alarm had been screaming for an hour, an equal companion to my mother's voice rising from the kitchen, both competing to drag me out of bed. I was supposed to be at work by ten, but the truth was that, I no longer cared. Deadlines, bosses, the endless grind. It all felt like background noise to a life I had stopped wanting to participate in.

My head hurting from last night's drinking session. Each pulse of pain was like a nail being hammered deeper into my skull. I stumbled into the shower, hoping the water might wash away more than just sweat and fatigue. But the moment my eyes closed, the images of the dream returned.

That dream. The same one that had begun haunting me weeks ago. I wouldn't have thought much of it. Dreams usually vanish like smoke at sunrise, but this one refused to let go. It clawed me awake night after night, until I began to wonder whether if I had really lost my mind.

People around me had started to notice. My distracted stares, the slips in my speech, the way I sometimes lost myself mid-conversation. They whispered, some even said it outright: *He's losing his mind.* Maybe they were right. But the truth was simpler, and far darker. I hadn't lost my mind. I had lost my reason to live.

Most nights, as I laid in bed staring into the darkness, I found myself whispering the same silent wish: *Let me not wake up tomorrow.* And each morning, when the alarm dragged me back into the world, disappointment struck deeper than relief.

Dressing up for work felt like dragging another skin on my present one. I opened the wardrobe and dug past a heap of clothes until my fingers touched the cold glass. The bottle of whiskey had been waiting there, hidden yet not hidden enough. I pulled it out, poured myself a large, and downed it in one burning gulp. That was breakfast.

From the kitchen drifted the low murmur of voices of my father's and mother's. His words weren't clear, but I didn't need clarity. I knew the subject. Me. It was always me these days.

Since his retirement earlier this year, he had been home every morning, watching the small failures of my routine stack one on top of the other. I often wondered which disappointed him more: the son who couldn't wake on time, or the man who didn't seem to care anymore.

I stepped into the living room, bike keys clenched in my fist like a shield. His eyes flicked up, just for a second, but I avoided them. I couldn't bear the weight of what they carried—concern, disapproval, maybe even pity Without a word, I slipped out the door. The sunlight felt too bright, too exposing, as if the whole world had seen me stumble.

The ride to work took half an hour—long enough for a guilt trip. It had become my favorite pastime, the only ritual that never failed. With every passing street, I rehearsed the same thoughts: how my parents deserved better and how I had failed them.

They hadn't asked for much. Just a son they could point to with pride, a son who carried their hopes forward. Instead, they got me—late, lost, and drifting. Other men my age were already rooted in careers, building families, collecting milestones to display like trophies. I, at twenty-seven, had only just stumbled into my first job, and most mornings I showed up half in my senses.

I told myself it didn't matter. The mask on my face, mandated by a pandemic, hid more than just my breath. It concealed the man behind it, the hollow beneath the skin. I barely spoke to anyone anyway. A few muttered good mornings, a polite goodbye, and I was gone. That was the extent of my social life.

The work itself wasn't the problem. I was competent, even reliable. The salary was decent enough. But my days blurred together, eight hours at a desk followed by the only part of my life that felt like mine: returning home, washing off the day, and going back out into the night, chasing whiskey until memory surrendered and sorrow drowned.

I never meant to live like this. Nobody does. Beneath the haze of whiskey and wasted mornings, I still carried the same simple wish: to see my parents happy, to see pride flicker in their eyes when they spoke of me.

It's not as if they cursed me or treated me with resentment. No, their words, sharp as they sometimes felt, were always meant for my good. I knew that. Perhaps that's what made the guilt heavier, harder to bear.

There was a time when I wasn't like this. A time when I was filled with fire, with dreams that felt larger than life. I wanted to stand tall, to represent my nation. I wanted to wipe away the lines of worry etched on my parents' faces. I wanted to love and be loved. I wanted to believe in that elusive promise—*happily ever after.*

But dreams have a way of unraveling, thread by thread, until all you're left with is the memory of once wanting. And for me, that unraveling began in a small city called NASHIK.

NASHIK,

To the world, Nashik was just another small city in Maharashtra, but to me, it was everything. It was where my dreams were born, long before the world taught me how fragile dreams could be. Nashik is not just a city—it is a passage through time. Within a few miles, you can travel through centuries. From the worn stone steps of ancient temples to the echo of footsteps on forts that once guarded kingdoms; from the narrow lanes lined with age-old houses to the open hills that watch silently over the city; and then, suddenly, to the glass façades of malls, the glow of neon lights, the pulse of a growing economy. Nashik grows restlessly, yet its roots cling stubbornly to history.

This land has carried myths and legends on its shoulders. The Godavari river, born in the Brahmagiri hills, still whispers stories from the *Ramayana*, for it is here, that Lord Rama, Sita, and Lakshmana once walked. The very name *Panchavati* breathes of exile and devotion, and every stone feels touched by something eternal. The forts that crown its hills—like Harihar and Trimbak—stand as quiet sentinels of a past long gone but never forgotten.

And yet, alongside this ancient rhythm, Nashik hums with the tune of modern ambition. Vineyards spread like green seas under the sun, earning the city its title as the wine capital of India. Industrial hubs rise where fields once lay, and new roads carve paths to a future that races ahead.

It is a city of contrasts—where prayer bells and factory sirens coexist, where history lingers in every corner, even as glass towers scrape for tomorrow's sky.

On the outskirts of Nashik, I lived in a joint family that stretched across generations—my parents, my older brother, my grandparents, two uncles, and two aunts all under the same roof. My father, the eldest of five siblings, carried the weight of both responsibility and pride.

We lived in a government quarter, a privilege earned by my grandfather, who had spent his life in service as a government employee. It was he who broke the chain of poverty for us, carving a path out of struggle through sheer will and discipline. Before my parents' marriage, the family had crowded into a small, fragile house, one that held more dreams than space. Education was the door my grandfather had chosen to knock upon, and it opened for us.

He believed fiercely in its power. To him, books were the truest inheritance he could offer. He made certain each of his children studied diligently, completed their chosen streams, and built careers that commanded respect. His vision was clear: no child of his would be bowed by poverty again.

I remember the routine he imposed with absolute clarity. Two hours of study in the afternoon, two more before dinner, followed by a review of what we had learned. The days were measured not by sunsets, but by lessons completed. Even now, he insists with his voice softer with age, but no less resolute that learning is the only ladder worth climbing.

Whenever the newspaper carried an advertisement for job vacancies, he would call me over, tapping the page with steady fingers, urging me to apply. And I always nodded, never refusing him. But deep inside, I carried a secret he never suspected—I rarely applied. I already knew what the results would be. Failure had become so familiar, I could predict it before I even began.

My childhood was stitched together with countless happy moments. Being the youngest in a large joint family, I was wrapped in affection, pampered at every turn. My brother received no less. He was the first grandson in both my parents' families, and for that alone he carried a special kind of importance. Together, we filled the house with noise. There was never a dull moment when we played; our laughter and quarrels collided endlessly, so much so that fighting became our second language. He excelled in sports, I in academics—a balance that life would later twist in unexpected ways.

Like his father before him, my father served in the government sector. A government job came with its security, its steady respect, but also with sacrifices that bent his back and stole his time. Every three years, he was transferred to a different district, and with each posting came the choice: to uproot us, or to leave us behind. He chose the latter—not out of neglect, but out of love. Constant relocation would have meant new homes, new schools, new worlds to adjust to every few years.

It would have unsettled our education, disrupted the fragile rhythm of our lives. So, it was decided, my brother, my mother, and I would remain in Nashik, while he carried his work and his loneliness elsewhere.

We grew up with him as a weekend presence. On Saturdays and Sundays, the house felt fuller, steadier, his voice filling the air like an anchor we didn't know we had been missing all week. Then, just as quickly, Mondays would arrive, and he would be gone again, his absence stretching across days like a shadow at the breakfast table.

My mother, like every Indian mother, was a force of care and endurance. She carried the house on her shoulders, feeding us, tending to my grandparents, keeping the household running like clockwork. And yet, she somehow always found the time to hover over us, making sure her two sons didn't grow up wild.

Of course, we tested her patience daily. My brother and I were partners in mischief, and whenever we pushed too far, discipline arrived in the form of a belt. It wasn't cruelty. It was her way of drawing the line, of making sure we didn't mistake her gentleness for weakness. Even now, I believe it was necessary. Without that discipline, the love might have been taken for granted.

Her mornings began long before ours. By the time she woke us, she had already finished her chores—sweeping, cooking, preparing tiffins, laying out uniforms. At 7:30 sharp, she would march us off to school, which was just a short walk away. Reaching school was never the problem; waking us up for it was the real battle.

Some of those belt lessons came in the early hours, when I refused to budge from bed. I would finally rise, stumble into the bathroom, gulp down milk or hurriedly chew a piece of breakfast, slip into my uniform, only to crawl back under the blanket. My body was dressed for school, but my heart clung stubbornly to sleep.

And in some ways, that habit never really left me. Even as an adult, rushing to the office, I found myself reliving the same struggle—half-awake, half-ready, chasing time while wishing for just a little more sleep.

In the 90's, homes like ours had only fragments of entertainment, and even those felt precious. We had a single television, connected to an old antenna that seemed to have a mind of its own. Owning a TV itself was a luxury; making it work was another story. On many evenings, my uncle would climb up to the roof, shaking the antenna in random directions while someone below shouted, *Thamb! Ata barobar aahe!"* Miraculously, the blurred figures on the screen would sharpen, and the world outside our modest home suddenly seemed closer.

There were only one or two channels to watch, but they were enough to bring the whole family together. Sunday mornings belonged to *Mahabharat*, when the streets outside grew quiet, as though the entire city paused to listen to the echoes of conch shells and the thunder of chariots. And when India played cricket, especially with Sachin Tendulkar at the crease, our living room transformed into a stadium. His name had already turned into a prayer across the country, and in our home too, it was spoken with awe.

Naturally, like every child of the 90's or perhaps of any era, my brother and I wanted to play like him. After weeks of begging and promises to study harder, my father finally gave in and bought us a bat. It was wooden, heavy, with a glossy red sticker plastered on both sides. For me, short and skinny as I was, it felt less like a bat and more like a log. I pleaded for a lighter one of my own, but my protests faded into silence. One bat was enough.

We played anyway tirelessly and feverishly. My brother's friends from the neighborhood joined, filling the narrow street outside our quarter with shouts and laughter. I was always the youngest, the weakest, and I didn't play well. Most days, I was pushed to the corner of the field, where the ball almost never came. Bowling and batting were privileges reserved for the older boys. My turn with the bat came only at the end, when everyone else had gotten out and only a few overs were left. It hurt, that quiet exclusion. But even so, I was grateful just to stand among them, to chase a ball once in a while, to feel like I belonged at least on the edges of the game.

The obsession with Sachin Sir and cricket was such that I looked for it in everything. Clothes, toys, notebooks, posters, stickers, trump cards, even packaged snacks. If it had even a faint trace of cricket on it, it became my prized possession.

Among all these, there was one little candy that stood above the rest. I can't recall how that candy tasted, or even how it looked. But to me, it wasn't just candy. It was magic wrapped in colorful paper. It cost only twenty-five paise, yet it fed my cricket fever more than anything else. Inside every wrapper was a sticker, and on those stickers were digits—runs. One might have a "1," another a "4" for a boundary, or a "6" for a mighty shot over the ropes. But there were also rare ones, the kind that made your heart race: special deliveries, iconic strokes, fielding achievements.

The rule was simple—collect stickers worth a hundred runs, complete a category, and you'd win a prize. And not just any prize, but real cricketing gear. For me, that meant one thing: a bat of my own.

I didn't care whether I could play well with it or not. All I wanted was to own that bat. Because the rule of cricket in every lane was clear and universal: *the one who owns the bat gets to play first.* Until then, my brother's bat had always ruled over me. But with my own bat, I dreamed of finally stepping in first, raising it high like Sachin, while the world waited for my shot.

The contest required an enrollment form to be filled and mailed through post. Once enrolled, every participant received a project book with neat little slots, waiting for the stickers to be pasted in their rightful place. And once the book was complete, it had to be mailed back. The promise was simple: fill the book, and win glory.

Thus began my quest. Four candies a day. That was the limit of my ambition and my pocket money. If life had given me the freedom and funds, I would have eaten an entire bucketful in one sitting. But a seven-year-old has neither the money nor the authority to live such grand dreams. So, every day, with coins clutched in my palm, I went to the local grocery shop, bought my four candies, and tore open their wrappers with trembling excitement. Each sticker felt like a lottery ticket.

As the days passed, the project book began to fill. I was inching closer to my dream, only three stickers away from the prize that mattered most—the bat. But with every sunset, the deadline crept nearer, and my patience wore thin. The impossible truth loomed over me: the bat might never be mine.

What I didn't notice, though, was that in my desperate hunt for the bat's stickers, I had unknowingly completed another set, one that guaranteed me a different prize. But how could I settle for less? The bat wasn't just wood and leather; it was my ticket to fame, my key to glory, my right to walk in and claim the first batting slot.

Yet, time was running out. And some prize, as my grandfather reminded me, was better than no prize at all. So, with a heavy heart and a lump in my throat, I chose surrender over hope. That afternoon, holding my grandfather's hand, I walked to the post office. With every step, I felt like I was carrying my broken dream. And when the parcel finally slid into the red postbox, it felt as though my bat had been buried there with it.

Weeks passed, and the postbox remained silent. Every afternoon I would run to the gate at the sound of the cycle bell, only to be disappointed. My prize, I knew, would arrive by post. Three weeks later, the wait finally ended. The doorbell rang, and before my mother could even reach the door, I had already sensed it—*this was the day.*

I sprinted, but she opened the door first. The postman handed over a small parcel. I didn't even let my mother hold it for long—I snatched it from her hands and darted inside, my heart hammering like I was running to chase down a ball at the boundary. The plastic tore away in seconds. I opened the box, my breath caught halfway in my throat, ready for the miracle. And then—

A pair of wicket-keeping gloves.

I froze. My hands held them, but my mind refused to. I had seen gloves like these on television, worn by men diving and catching with style. But me? I didn't even know what to do with them. At home, our wicket-keeper was the wall behind the old wooden plank we used as stumps. The gloves felt grand, important… yet completely useless.

I was blank. Empty. This wasn't the bat, this wasn't the glory, this wasn't the dream.

A few days went by. Then came a lazy Sunday morning, the kind where the sun was soft, and the air smelled of wet mud from last night's watering. Me and my brother were playing cricket in the backyard, with grandfather bowling in his steady rhythm. I looked at the gloves lying nearby and thought—*why not give them a chance?* I slid my hands inside, struggling. They were far too big for my tiny fingers. I could barely fit one glove properly, so I wore it only on my right hand and went to stand behind grandfather.

My brother hit one ball, hard and quick, sailing just above my height. On instinct, I lifted my gloved hand—without any real hope of stopping it. And then—magic.

The ball thudded into the glove and stuck there. For a moment, time froze. I just stared at the white ball resting inside that red-and-black glove. It felt unreal, like I had unlocked some hidden power.

From that day on, those gloves were no longer useless. They were my treasure. I never took them off whenever we played cricket. To me, they weren't just gloves anymore—they were proof that I too could belong in the game.

CHAPTER 2
CHASING DREAMS

TIME WENT BY. Enter new millennium. New millennium bought a new home. Grandpa got retired in the year 2000. We left the government quarter and shifted in our new home. Our own home which my parents were planning to buy for many years. In 2003 my brother had his 10th board exams. Our father had promised us that he would enroll us in a summer cricket coaching camp if my brother passed the finals with good marks. And that my brother delivered. I was just eleven years old. I had never been so much excited for anything till then.

First day at the camp. My heart was pounding with excitement and nervousness. Wearing the whites for the first time. I was ready before time. My mother was looking at me in shock and somewhat anger.

"You don't seem this much eager while going to school". said mom.

Dad took us to the ground on his scooter, the morning wind brushing against my face like a silent cheerleader. The moment we arrived, my eyes widened—nearly fifty boys stood scattered across the field, buzzing with energy. It felt like stepping into another world.

We were quickly divided into two groups: the older ones, tall and confident, and the younger ones—boys like me, still testing their first steps in this world of cricket. I, of course, was sent with the younger group.

And then I saw it for the first time. The Red Cherry. The leather ball, shining under the morning sun, looked like treasure to me. Until then, cricket had always meant rubber balls or tennis balls. But this—this was the real deal. My hands itched to touch it, but that honor wasn't for the first day.

In any camp, they said, you had to earn your way to cricket. The beginning was all about the body. Running, stretching, push-ups, flexibility drills, hand-eye coordination. We formed a semicircle on the grass, and an older student tossed an old, scarred leather ball toward us, one by one, to practice catching. The ball felt heavy, alive, as it smacked into my palms.

For a few days, this was our routine. No matches, no batting, no bowling—only the basics. My eyes often drifted toward the older boys, who had already begun playing in the nets. Their laughter, the sound of bat striking ball, the shouts of "bowled!" made me burn with jealousy. I wanted to be there, not here.

But then, everything changed.

After about a week, our coach gathered us in a circle and asked each of us what we liked doing most.

"Batting," said one.

"Fast bowling," another answered, puffing his chest.

Almost everyone wanted the glory roles.

When my turn came, I felt a sudden calm. "I like being behind the stumps," I said.

The coach raised his eyebrows, perhaps surprised. "A keeper, hmm? That's rare."

And that was it. That moment became the quiet turning point of my life. From that day onward, the gloves were mine. I wore them with pride, and for the next ten years, I never let go.

One month had passed. I was doing good and learning new things everyday. My brother was doing even better. He was now the opening batsmen for the senior's team. There was an upcoming tournament for which we were preparing. The thrill of playing a real cricket match excited me. The first match very special for me. We won that match quite easily. Our team did quite well in that tournament. We lost in semi-finals. It was still good for first timers.

Summer camp lasted for two months, and just like that, it was time for school again. But something had changed. Walking alone to school felt strange now—my brother had moved on to college, and suddenly, I was the only one in uniform at home.

I couldn't wait for the first day back. Not because of studies, not because of teachers, but because I wanted to tell my friends everything.

"So, what did you do in vacations?" I asked my friend.

"I visited my grandparents" he said.

"And what did you do?" I asked another friend.

"I went on a trip with my parents." said another friend.

"You know what I did. I learned how to play cricket with leather ball. I even played in a tournament." I said.

It felt awesome to brag about the camp, but soon reality set in that the summer was over. Yet, all I could think about was cricket. School, books, even homework seemed like background noise; cricket had taken center stage in my mind.

When I told my parents I wanted to join the school cricket team, their faces carried the same concern that every Indian parent has—*"What about studies?"* But my grades had stayed steady, and that consistency became my strongest argument. Reluctantly, yet lovingly, they agreed.

I went for the trials of the under-14 team with a pounding heart. To my relief, getting in wasn't too difficult. Still, I was the youngest, just a boy in sixth grade among seniors from seventh and eighth. At first, I thought I would be treated like the little one, a tagalong. But to my surprise, my teammates welcomed me as an equal. On the field, age mattered less; effort and spirit mattered more.

That year, I played only two games, but those two felt like entire tournaments to me. Every run I saved, every cheer from the sidelines—it all stitched itself into my memory. I was learning what it meant to be part of a team: the joy of celebrating someone else's success, the discipline of playing for the whole rather than the self, the invisible thread of camaraderie that binds eleven players together.

And the results spoke for themselves. We won every interschool match that season. Even though my role was small, the happiness it gave me was enormous. Pride swelled in me—not just because we had won, but because I had finally stepped onto the path I had always dreamed of.

Things at home were changing, and so was life around me. Out went the old antenna, and in came the cable connection. Suddenly, the little black-and-white world of one or two channels exploded into colors, stories, and endless possibilities. For me, it meant more cricket matches to watch, more replays to study, more heroes to idolize. For the ladies of the house, it meant daily soaps every evening, a brand-new ritual that kept them hooked to the screen. The living room became a battlefield of remote control, but in the end, everyone was happy—we had something for all.

Around the same time, my friend Karan moved in just two blocks away. His arrival changed my world as much as cable television had. With him, I had a new partner-in-crime, someone who shared my excitement, my games, and sometimes even my punishments. Childhood suddenly felt bigger, brighter, and a lot more fun.

That year everything changed for me. I wasn't just a filler in the team anymore. I played every game, kept well behind the stumps, and even my batting had started to improve. Being treated as an equal by the senior boys gave me a new sense of belonging.

The tournament, though, tested our patience. August rains turned our ground into a pool, delaying matches for weeks. Maybe that's when my dislike for rain truly began. Watching it steal away the game I loved.

When play finally resumed, our new captain, the star batsman, led us smoothly through the group stages. My small contributions with the bat felt bigger than they were. But cricket can be unforgiving—we lost in the semi-final. This time, the defeat stung deeper, because now I knew what it meant to give yourself completely to the game.

Next year, eight grade. Things were good at home. Out went old Television and in came a bigger color television. The Men in Blue looked bigger and brighter now. MS Dhoni had announced his arrival at international level with 148 of 123 balls in a test match against Pakistan.

Last year of playing for the school under 14 team. I couldn't wait for the matches to begin. We began practice sessions earlier that year. One day during our practice, our sports teacher called everyone in the gym. Senior team was also present. He introduced new players selected during trails. New players were selected by Sports teacher and Captain of the senior team only. He also introduced the new captain of the under-14 team. Everyone applauded. It's not that the thought had not passed through my head, but hearing my name came to me a bit shocking. I was happy and excited to do my best as a captain.

The back pages of my notebook slowly turned into cricket fields. Each page had a new diagram, different field placements, initials of players, and strategies for every bowler. I took my role as captain seriously. With the bat too, the team needed me to deliver. Whenever doubts crept in, I turned to the senior team's captain—my mentor in many ways. It was his idea that I should open the innings. I hesitated at first, but gave it a try. The first game as opener was a struggle, but I bounced back in the next one with a steady contribution.

We kept winning, cruising through the group stages. Soon, we were in the semi-finals. Last year's defeat at this very stage still haunted me, but this time we pulled through. Into the finals—my very first year as captain. I was thrilled. Winning the cup as skipper would be the perfect ending.

But the final was a different story. The opposition dominated us in every department. We were completely outplayed. When it was over, I walked off with my head down. The loss stung deeper than anything before. It felt personal. I blamed myself, replaying moments in my head. For the first time, defeat left a bitter taste I couldn't swallow.

Three months had passed, yet the sting of that defeat refused to fade. It showed in my studies. My grades sank lower with each exam, and eighth grade turned out to be my worst academic year. Passing with such a poor percentage was hard for me, but even harder for my parents to digest. To them, it was simple: cricket had made me reckless.

Their solution was immediate—coaching classes for the next year. I hated it. I felt like an outcast, sitting among students who seemed more focused, more driven. But I had no choice. If I wanted to continue cricket, I had to raise my grades. Life became a cycle of early morning school, then classes straight after. Cricket barely found space in my day, and that frustrated me.

As the interschool tournament approached, I clung to it as my only escape, my chance to redeem myself. But nature played its own game. Heavy rains and storms washed away every match. The monsoon stretched on, cruelly long, and with it went an entire year of cricket. Sometimes, I even wondered if my parents had prayed for this.

With no cricket left to lean on, I buried myself in studies. It was the only way forward. By the end of the year, my grades showed some recovery—not great, but better. Next year awaited, and with it, a bigger test than any cricket match I had played.

CHAPTER 3

SO CLOSE YET SO FAR

TENTH GRADE HAD arrived like a storm. Books piled higher than ever, and every teacher carried the same sermon: *"This is the most important year of your life."* Yet, I wasn't ready to let go of cricket. Leading the side in my final year was a responsibility I couldn't run away from.

Balancing both wasn't easy. Mornings began with school, afternoons were swallowed by coaching classes, and evenings were reserved for cricket practice. By the time I got home, I was too tired to even glance at my textbooks. Still, I somehow managed.

Then came the day that shook me.

After practice, as I was collecting the stumps and packing up the kit, I saw my father entering the ground. He never visited. He walked straight towards the school gym, where my coach was seated.

I lingered at a distance, pretending to tie my shoelaces, but my eyes were fixed on them. I couldn't hear what they were saying, but their expressions told me enough. My father spoke with seriousness, his arms folded, his forehead creased. My coach listened quietly, nodding every now and then. The conversation lasted only a few minutes, but to me, it felt like an eternity.

When it ended, both of them glanced in my direction. My father gave me a faint smile—one that looked more like concern than encouragement—and then left. My coach didn't call me over. He simply picked up his clipboard and walked towards the dressing room. Their conversation ended after a few minutes, but before I could even breathe a sigh of relief, I saw my father walk towards the principal's office. That was it. The final nail in the coffin. Not only would I miss the tournament, I was certain I wouldn't be playing a single game ever again.

That night, I couldn't sleep. My mind replayed the scene again and again. What could they have talked about? I didn't need anyone to tell me. I knew. My father must have asked him to drop me from the team. It made perfect sense. For months, he had been worried about my studies, warning me not to lose focus. Now, he had probably taken matters into his own hands.

Word spread quickly among my teammates. We were all downcast that day, the air heavy with silence. To forget our sorrows, we decided to escape to the samosa stall near school.

"My dear friends, it has been an honor playing alongside you for our school team. The time has come for me to leave this game of cricket. I never thought this day would arrive, but life has its own plans. You must continue without me and win every single match for our school. I'll cheer for you from the sidelines. Thank you for your love and support. And now, I declare my retirement from all forms of cricket. If anyone wants to say anything, please speak now."

Ravi raised his hand.

"Yes, Ravi?" I asked.

"Can I have one more samosa?" he said.

"Sure. And Akash, there's no need to cry," I said.

"I'm not crying! This samosa is too hot. Can I get something to drink?" he replied, his eyes watering.

"Go ahead. Anyone else want to say something or need something?" I asked.

So that was all for my grand retirement party. We laughed, but deep inside I was breaking. I wanted nothing more than to lead my team to victory in the finals, one last attempt at glory.

That night, however, laughter gave way to silence. I didn't speak to anyone. My parents didn't bother to ask what was wrong, and their silence felt like betrayal.

How could they do this to me? I kept asking myself. I wasn't the brightest in class, but I wasn't failing either. I was balancing studies and cricket the best I could. And yet, it seemed like none of that mattered.

Next day I reached school barely five minutes before the gate closed. Normally, I would arrive an hour early for practice, but not today. I could see the boys practicing in one corner of the ground. I avoided looking at them directly and walked to class with my head hung low, my chest heavy with jealousy.

During the break, as we ate from our lunch boxes, Ravi came looking for me.

"Sir has asked you to come meet him in the gym," Ravi said.

"For what?" I asked, startled.

"How would I know? Ooh, you brought parathas today?" Ravi grinned.

I finished my meal with some help from Ravi and together we went to the gym.

"Sir, you asked for me?" I said hesitantly.

"Yes," he replied. "Why weren't you on the ground today?"

Why was he asking me that? He knew why I hadn't shown up.

"Sir… my father—" I began.

"Your father is a good man," he interrupted. "He cares for your future. And you're a good kid too, with great potential. That is why I vouched for you. I've requested your father to let you play, and I assured him that you'll study harder and bring back good grades. Once the matches are over, I want you and all the other boys to focus on exams. Don't you dare let me down. Now go, and don't be late for practice tomorrow."

"Yes, sir. Thank you so much," I managed to say. My heart was bursting with joy. I wanted to jump, to scream, to run around in circles, but I held it in. After all, I was still in school.

That night at home, I wanted to hug my father but couldn't gather enough courage. Still, the happiness on my face gave me away. When I told my mother what had happened, she smiled knowingly, like she had been in on it all along.

The season began with great excitement and energy. We were confident that this time we would go all the way. Match after match, we cruised through with strong performances. Our bowlers, especially Ravi, were at their absolute best.

Ravi was a big bloke. Almost six feet tall and a bit on the heavier side, but that didn't stop him from bowling fast in-swinging deliveries that rattled batsmen. Ram, my steady opening partner, was someone I could always rely on. Vivek, one of the most talented players I've ever known, was not just a teammate but a close friend for life. Akash, with his clever off-spinners, often turned games in our favor. And of course, Ravi again, who was impossible to ignore. There were others too, but these names shine brightest in my memory.

Then came the day of the final match. The match I had played out in my mind a million times. Every strategy, every field setting, every game plan was ready to be tested in reality. We were fired up, buzzing with nervous excitement.

I walked out for the toss. There was one record I hated about myself: I had never won a single toss in my life. And true to form, I made the wrong call again. The opposition chose to bowl first. Ironically, we had wanted to bowl first too. Fate had other plans.

First Innings.

Me and Ram started the innings.

"Let's start slowly. It's a twenty-five over game and we will bat through till the last." I said to Ram.

Five over had gone, score was 26/0. It was the sixth over and Ram tried to play an away ball. He edged and it went to the keeper. The keeper made no mistake and our first wicket had fallen. In came Vivek. For the next few overs, we decided to play safe and not let any wicket fall.

Score - 59/1 after 11 overs.

Almost half the innings was over. With both batsmen set, it was time to get some quick runs. For the next five overs we played some aggressive cricket. Vivek was a naturally aggressive batsman.

Score – 109/1 after 16 overs.

Into the seventeenth over. I played a lofted delivery straight past the bowler to long off. Fielder was placed deep and two runs were possible. We took the first run fast and it was Vivek's call for the second as he was going to run towards the danger end. He called for the run and as I turned after completing the first, and suddenly I ran into the bowler. We both fell down. Vivek had already reached the bowling end. I quickly recollected myself and ran towards the batting end. But it didn't matter. The ball had reached the batting end and bells were taken off by the keeper with me yards away. The leg umpires finger went up and my last innings for the school team came to an anti-climatic end. My innings ended on 53 runs.

Score – 110/2 after 16.2 overs.

After my wicket things started to go down the hill for us. Wickets kept falling from one end like dominoes. Vivek kept his head cool and kept the score board ticking, but eventually he got out while playing a lofted shot straight to the fielder at mid-wicket.

Score - 141/7 after 22 overs.

Last few overs went silently with Ravi hitting two boundaries in the last over which made us all stand and dance in excitement. We reached a defendable score. We could have finished better but still we had runs on the board to defend.

Score – 161/8 after 25 overs.

162 runs required to win from 150 balls.

Our Sir gave us all the right instructions and motivation which we needed. "Don't let them any easy runs. Be on your toes. Do not give any extras. That means no wide balls, no no-balls and no over-throws. Take all the chances that come your way. If you do all this you are going to win. Good luck boys. Let's win this".

Second Innings.

First ball – outside off, medium pace. The batsman let it go. Straight into my gloves.

Second ball – same line, a touch quicker. Again, left alone.

Third ball – a little fuller. The batsman leaned in and caressed it through the covers. The ball raced to the boundary. Silence from us.

Fourth ball – good length, same channel. The drive came, but missed everything. I went up in appeal, but the umpire was unmoved.

Fifth ball – fuller again, but this time Ravi made it swing back in. The batsman, stuck between drive and defense, dragged it onto his stumps.

The bail lit up, the roar was deafening. First wicket gone.

Sixth ball – defended by the batsman.

Score: 4/1 after 1 over.

The next few overs were tense, cat and mouse. We took wickets at intervals, but they kept the run rate just ahead of us. In the 10th over, Vivek steamed in and hurled a nasty bouncer. The batsman went for a pull, top-edged it high. The ball ballooned in the air, and I steadied myself under it. Safe catch.

Score: 64/4 after 10 overs.

From the 11th to the 15th, we shut them down completely. No boundaries, only singles and doubles. Frustration was written across the set batsman's face. He was their only hope, and we had marked him.

Score: 96/4 after 15 overs.

We needed a breakthrough. Yogesh provided one. He had this gift, off-cutters, leg-cutters, and a devilish slower ball. In the 17th over, he tossed in a full slower one. The batsman went for glory, missed, and was struck plumb in front. The umpire's finger went up instantly. The boys erupted.

Then again in the 19th, Yogesh tempted another batsman with a fuller ball outside off. Mistimed, straight to mid-off.

Score: 125/6 after 20 overs.

Akash had finished his five overs. Rajesh too, though expensive. Sam's off-spin had no bite today. That left me with five overs to split between Ravi, Vivek, and Yogesh. Ravi struggled with the old ball, but I had no choice. He had to take one more over. Then Vivek and Yogesh would finish.

I tossed the ball to Ravi for the 21st.

First ball – pitched up, driven hard, but straight back to him. Dot ball.

Second – fuller again, this time worked between midwicket and long-on. Two runs.

Third – attempted yorker, missed length. Half-volley. The bat swung clean, the ball soared over his head. Six. Opposition supporters found their voice. Ravi's shoulders tensed.

I walked up, put a hand on his back. "Breathe. Focus. Stick to the plan. Full and outside off."

The next two balls – controlled. Singles only.

Last ball – a disaster. Ravi strayed on the pads, glanced fine past me. No fielder behind. Four runs.

That over hurt. fourteen runs from it. My heart screamed, but I forced myself to stay calm. The match was alive.

The next two overs were a masterclass. Vivek and Yogesh bowled with fire, squeezing every run. Only 11 came off 12 balls.

Score: 150/6 after 23 overs.

12 runs in 12 deliveries. We were desperate for a wicket. Vivek in his final over of the match. First three deliveries went for two singles and a double. Fourth ball of the over. Short length delivery on the off side. Batsmen hit it towards deep-point and started running. There was a mix-up between both batsmen and there was our chance to bounce back in the game. The batsman at the striker's end wanted the second run but the other batsman refused. Before the batsman could turn around, fielder had already thrown the ball towards me and I made no mistake in collecting the ball and lodging the bells off. There was our ray of shining light. My dream was still intact. We were ecstatic and knew that we could win it from here. Only one run came in next two deliveries.

If we bowled and fielded perfectly, we could win. I urged my teammates to be on their toes, every muscle ready to pounce. Yogesh had bowled brilliantly all match, taking two wickets and choking their runs, but defending six in the final over could shake anyone.

Last over. Six runs required.

First ball: Dot.

Second ball: A single.

Third ball: Driven into the gap for two.

Equation: 3 runs from 3 balls.

The fourth ball—fuller length. The batsman threw his hands at it, but it went straight to covers. They hesitated for a single and turned back.

3 from 2.

The pressure was visible on the batsman's face, and Yogesh was doing everything he could to stay calm. Then came the mistake—a wide ball. The equation shrank to two from two. I ran to Yogesh, put a hand on his shoulder.

"Don't worry. Just full outside off. Don't let him get under it. Either he'll miss or lob it."

He nodded. Fifth delivery, bowled exactly as planned. The batsman swung, missed.

2 required from the final ball.

I pulled everyone inside the circle, except long-off and deep cover. Yogesh charged in. He wanted to repeat the same ball but missed his length—full toss. The batsman swung hard, edged it, and the ball flew.

That day I learnt a valuable lesson. Timing is most important thing in life. You might do everything that can be done. You put all the hard work with all the dedication to achieve your goal. But if Time isn't in your favor, there is nothing much you can do. The irony was that the batsman didn't time the ball well. If he had timed the ball with middle of the bat, it would have gone straight to the fielder. But it was his time. His timing was perfect to get the edge of the bat. And as the ball sailed past the boundary line, the opposition team erupted in celebration.

I stood still for a moment. The weight of the moment finally sinked in and I collapsed on the ground. Two runs. One ball. And it slipped away. My heart was broken, not just with the loss, but with the realization that this was the last time I was going to be a part of this team. The noise around me faded into a dull hum in my ears. All I could hear was the echo of years of hard work and every moment spent with my teammates. All the moments that had led to this day. It felt like a sting on the chest or a frog stuck in my throat. Not just from the defeat, but the fact that I won't get another chance to set things right. I started sobbing like a child. It felt like the end of world. My teammates came running towards me. My body lying on the ground like a corpse. Ravi lifted me up in both his arms and took me to the stands.

Days passed but the memories of that day were still fresh in my mind. As if it was yesterday. Time went by and the final exams were approaching. I had promised everyone that I would study hard and achieve good grades in the board exams. And just like that it was time for the last day of school. The ground looked emptier than ever. Everything started to come back to me. My first trials for the team. The day I played my first game. The day Sir announced me as the captain. The jokes we shared with each other. I took a walk along the ground to feel the air for one last time.

All the team members gathered together on the field for one last time together. There was the laughter that I cherished for past few years, but it was softer now, laced with the burden of goodbyes. Some of which forever, never to meet again. One thing I wouldn't miss before leaving school that day was to meet our Sir.

"Sir."

"Yes. Aditya, come inside. How are you feeling."

"Fine Sir."

"How is the preparation for exams?"

"Good."

"Still thinking about the game?"

"No Sir."

"You will get more opportunities in future. Playing for the school was the first step. The world is bigger than this with many opportunities for the one who is willing to work hard. I have been teaching in this school for fifteen years now and I remember only few students who share your passion. Whether you continue playing cricket or choose different career path, I know you will succeed in life. And always take care of your parents. Now go and meet me after the results."

"Thank you, Sir. Good bye." I was speechless for a moment. Those words meant a lot for me.

Funny thing about board exams is that it haunts parents of the students more than the students themselves. So was the case at our home. No television for anyone. Everybody at home was tensed that whether I will pass the exams or not. Mother praying in the morning before every paper. Dad waking up before everyone and asking me all sorts of questions before leaving to the exam center.

"Have you packed everything". Asked my father.

"Yes dad."

"Writing pad?"

"Yes."

"Hall ticket?"

"Yes."

"Eat your breakfast quickly so that you will reach the center before time and don't be nervous." Said Mom.

"I am not nervous."

"Take blessings of God before leaving the home."

"Yes mom."

My dad took me to the exam center on our scooter. He had taken leave from work till my exams were over. He would stop at the gate, looking at me until I entered my block and be back before the end time.

The exams were quite easier than I expected, especially since I had not studied as much or as well as the other students.

"How was the paper?" After every subject paper my mother asked me the same question.

And I answered the same. "Good."

"How come you give the same answer every time? Karan's mother told me that today's paper was tough."

"That's because I am smarter than him."

She tried to glare at me, but a smile escaped anyway.

It was results day, and the whole house was tense. Results were to be declared online, and Dad had asked his friend who owned a cyber café to check and call as soon as they were out.

At around 11:10 a.m., Dad's phone rang. He stepped outside to answer, leaving me and Mom staring at him through the doorway, our hearts thudding. His face gave nothing away. All we heard was a quiet "Thank you" before he disconnected the call and walked back toward us.

I braced myself for the worst.

"Eighty percent," Dad said at last.

Relief washed over me. Mom's eyes welled with tears of happiness, and my brother sprinted to the sweet shop to bring back boxes for everyone. It was a happy surprise for the whole family. Even I couldn't believe it. I would have never imagined scoring that much, let alone passing.

The phone didn't stop ringing. Relatives, friends, everyone wanted to hear the news. The pride in my father's voice as he told people that his son had passed with first class—that was the greatest feeling of my life. Sweets were shared across the colony.

One neighbor even teased me, "What's the secret? How did you even pass? All you ever did was play cricket""

That night, Dad took us all to the fanciest restaurant in the city. Everyone was smiling, laughing, full of joy.

It was the last time I hugged my father.

The last time I saw pride in their eyes.

The last time I made them happy.

CHAPTER 4

CHASING THE LIGHT

THE CLOUDS GREW denser, swallowing everything into a white void. Through the haze, I saw someone falling below me. His body tumbling faster and faster, the ground pulling him in. At this speed, I wouldn't be able to catch him. Yet he didn't struggle. It was as if he had taken a leap of faith. But I had to try. I forced my body forward, pushing through the air to close the gap.

"Hey! Can you hear me? Slow down if you can. I'll reach you—just grab my hand when I do! Do you hear me? I'm trying to save you. Hey… who are you?"

The voice faded into silence.

My phone buzzed. Four missed calls glared at me before the fifth finally pulled me out of sleep. Karan's name flashed across the screen. It was 11:30 on a Sunday.

"What do you want? Why are you disturbing me in the morning?" I groaned.

"It's almost afternoon," Karan snapped. "Get ready quick. Bharat's father had a heart attack. They've taken him to the hospital. Pick me up in ten." He cut the call.

I threw on clothes and was about to leave when Mom stopped me.

"Where are you going? At least eat something."

"Bharat's dad is in the hospital. Karan and I are going."

"Oh… I hope everything's fine. Tell his mother I asked."

I nodded and rushed out. On the way, I picked up Karan. At the hospital, Bharat was inside the doctor's cabin. We waited outside, restless, until he came out.

"Everything alright?" Karan asked quickly.

Bharat shook his head. "No. Not really. They've put him in ICU."

"What happened exactly?" I asked.

"Last night, around midnight, he had chest pain. He told my mother, and she woke me up. I tried to talk to him, but he started gasping for air. I rushed to get my uncle downstairs, and we drove him straight to "What did the doctor say?" I asked.

Bharat exhaled slowly, his eyes red. "His vitals aren't good… blood levels are very low."

Karan leaned forward. "If you need anything, please tell us."

"It's fine for now. Thank you."

"Where's your mother?" Karan asked gently.

"I sent her home this morning with my uncle. She didn't rest the entire night."

"And tonight? Who's going to stay?" I asked.

"She insists on staying, but I think it's better if she gets some rest."

"We'll stay with you," I said firmly.

Bharat shook his head. "You really don't have to."

"We're not asking," Karan cut in. "We'll be here. If you need anything."

Later that night, Karan and I sat in my car in the hospital parking lot. I had brought a bottle of whiskey, and the burn of the first glass was already settling in my chest.

"You want some?" I asked, holding the bottle out.

Karan shook his head. "No. Don't you think you should cut down?"

"I'm fine."

He sighed. "It's been months now. You should move on. She's living her life, bro. Why are you still torturing yourself?"

"I said I'm fine," I snapped.

"Do you think we like seeing you like this? You were supposed to be.."

"Karan, please. Can we not?" I cut him off, sharper than I intended.

"Fine," he muttered, turning away.

I poured another glass. The silence between us grew heavy, almost louder than words. Finally, I pushed the bottle towards him. "If you're not going to talk, at least have a drink."

He hesitated, then poured himself a glass.

I stared at the windshield, voice low. "Lately I've been having this dream. Same one, almost every night. A guy falling from a bridge. Sometimes he jumps, suicide maybe. I go after him, try to catch him, but no matter what I do, I never reach him. Last night was different though… for the first time, I saw his face. He was just a boy."

Karan turned to me, eyes narrowing with concern. "Listen, brother… I know you don't want to hear this, but you need help. Real help. Having dreams like that isn't normal. Let us be there for you. Maybe counselling. It might actually help."

We were talking when Bharat came to check on us.

"You want some?" I asked, holding the bottle out.

"Are you crazy? My father is in the ICU and you're asking me to drink?"

"Fine, don't drink. But why are you out here?" I asked.

"My father is asleep. An emergency patient just came in—bike accident. Young boy. His parents were crying, chaos everywhere. I couldn't stay there long, so I came to check on you two. Seems like you're having fun," Bharat said.

"It was his idea. He brought the bottle," Karan said, pointing at me.

I stepped outside the car to smoke. Karan and Bharat shared a look, thinking I didn't notice. I handed Bharat a cigarette.

"I don't know if he'll make it," he said quietly.

"Don't talk like that. He'll be fine. Everything will be alright," I tried to reassure him.

"Last night, when my father became unconscious, it shook the ground beneath me," Bharat said, voice trembling. "We think we're grown-ups, ready to face any challenge… but there's no courage in the world for seeing your loved ones in pain. I just saw a mother and father cry for their son. The boy was drunk while driving. I saw my mother almost faint at the sight of my father. I'm not here to tell you what to do. You were always the best among us, and I think you still are. You've supported us through the worst. You failed hard, yes—but you never gave up. So why now? Stop treating yourself like this. If not for you, then do it for your parents. Take care of them while they're still here."

Twelfth board exam result day -

"I kept shouting my lungs out to you. Please study Adi, please study. I even enrolled you in the best coaching classes in the city.

And this is your outcome. Which college will give you admission." Dad kept screaming at me.

Twelfth board results were out and I had just scored fifty percent. My father was furious and my mother had not talked with me since morning.

"Physics – 39, Mathematics – 37, Chemistry – 41. You are not even eligible for engineering. What are you going to do? Tell me Adi, what are you going to do in future? I work hard so that I could give you a better life than what I had. But you have no value of your parent's sentiments."

At that moment my dad's mobile rang. Some relative were calling to ask about my results. My dad looked at the phone and then he looked at me angrily. I kept my head down in shame until he stopped scolding me. After few hours the storm had calmed a bit. But the tension was still in the air. Dad was answering every call and telling them calmy that his son has just passed the exams by minimum margin. I felt really guilty to let him down. It's not that I had not studied but science was not my cup of tea. I couldn't understand the concepts of physics or chemistry no matter how hard I tried.

"Pappa. I am sorry. I know I should have done better. I tried to study but I couldn't understand much." I tried to explain him.

"You have barely passed in the exam. You promised me you'd balance cricket and studies." Dad said.

"And I really tried, but I failed. I am sorry."

"Sorry is not going to change your marks. Think about your future. Will cricket feed you if things don't work out? The world isn't as kind as you think. Without education you won't have anything to fall back on."

"But if I give up cricket now, I'll regret it forever. Please believe in me dad." I tried to explain.

"Believing is one thing. Being blind is another. You won't understand how much we worry about you."

A long silence followed after. He looked at the result sheet, visibly disappointed, set it on the table and left the room. I stood there frozen, torn between guilt and stubbornness. I couldn't explain how much I wanted to succeed as a player. I did understand that he was not wrong for worrying about me.

Two years passed since that day. I had failed the first year my Bachelor's degree in commerce, mostly because of clashes with cricket matches, but I managed to pass the next year and move on. Surprisingly, Dad didn't react as he had before. Perhaps he was exhausted from repeating the same warnings, or maybe he had finally accepted that I was wired differently.

On the cricket field, I was thriving. I was captaining my college team and my club side, also securing a permanent place on the district team. Every match felt like a chance to prove myself, to live the dreams I had nurtured since my first day at summer camp. Academic setbacks seemed distant whenever I held the bat or slipped on the gloves.

One afternoon, during district team practice, I saw my father walking onto the ground. My heart skipped a beat. It had been a long time since he had shown up at one of my matches or practice sessions. I felt a strange mix of pride and anxiety. Pride that he cared enough to come, anxiety about what he might think of me now.

He walked straight to the coach and started asking about my performance. I was standing close enough to hear their conversation.

"Sir, how is he doing? Is he playing well?" Dad asked, his eyes scanning me playing in the nets.

The coach smiled, then nodded thoughtfully. "Your son is an excellent wicket-keeper. Quick reflexes, great awareness behind the stumps. But," he added, hesitating slightly, "sometimes he gets a bit too eager while batting. Plays the wrong shot in crucial moments. But the potential is enormous. With guidance and focus, he can become one of the best."

I felt my chest tighten. Yes, I had struggled with balancing cricket and studies, and yes, I had made mistakes on the field and off it, but the coach had seen my potential. And now, hearing it from him in front of my father… it felt like a small victory.

I looked at my dad, expecting the usual stern expression, but instead, I saw something different. A softening, a quiet pride. He still cared, even after all my failures and stubbornness.

I clenched my fists in silent determination. I would prove to him, and to myself, that I could succeed. Not just in cricket, but in life. I pushed myself harder than ever before. Early mornings, long nets, extra fitness sessions.

The club matches were my highlight with the season just starting. In the next three matches, I scored two centuries. The first one felt like a release—every stroke, every run, proof that all those hours in the nets were paying off. The second century was even sweeter, because I could feel my decision-making improving, my patience at the crease becoming second nature. Those games weren't just numbers, they were statements. I was here, I could perform, I could lead.

I also got the chance to play for the university team that year. When the state probables list came out, I was devastated to see I had just missed it. That pang of disappointment hit hard, but it didn't crush me. Instead, I felt a renewed focus. I had seen my potential, and now it was about refining it, pushing my limits, and being ready for the next year.

I knew I couldn't control the outcomes, only my effort and preparation. And if I kept working the way I had been, next year would be mine. I would be ready.

It was the start of my final year of college, and I could feel that this year was going to be different. Not just because it was the last year of my degree, but because something in the air felt… different. There was a subtle excitement I couldn't quite place. Maybe it was the shot at state selection, or maybe it was something else.

I was at the college practice nets one morning. The sun was warm, the smell of fresh-cut grass in the air, and the sound of leather hitting willow filled the open ground. I was so focused that I didn't notice anyone approaching… until I did.

A girl was walking past the nets, a stack of books clutched to her chest. She had those round glasses on, which screamed nerd. She moved quietly, almost as if she were trying not to disturb the world around her. Her eyes were on the ground, her steps measured, and she glanced briefly at the practice before continuing toward the library.

Something about her caught my attention. She wasn't loud, or flashy, or trying to get noticed. She just… existed in her own space. The way she held herself, the little tilt of her head as she adjusted the books in her arms, even the soft swing of her bag, all felt oddly mesmerizing. I felt a strange pull, a curiosity I hadn't expected.

I tried to focus on my practice, but my eyes kept drifting back to her as she walked away. There was a quiet confidence about her, but also a shyness that made her seem… different from everyone else around.

Later, when I mentioned it to Rajeev during a break, he chuckled. 'Oh, that's the new girl. First-year. Super shy. Maybe from a conservative family.'

Something about her made me want to know more. I couldn't stop thinking about her even as I returned to my nets, the ball in my hand suddenly feeling clumsier than ever.

Over the next few days, I found myself scanning the library path every time I came to practice. She seemed to appear at the same time, moving quietly between classes and the library. Sometimes I would see her sitting on the bench under a tree, absorbed in a book, completely unaware of the world around her.

I tried to focus on my batting, but my mind kept drifting back to her. The way she tucked a strand of hair behind her ear, the soft concentration on her face, the slight smile when she noticed something in her book. It was frustrating. I couldn't figure out why someone I had barely spoken to was suddenly occupying so much space in my thoughts.

One afternoon, as I was wrapping up practice, I saw her again. This time she paused, adjusting her bag, glancing in my direction. My heart skipped a beat. Did she notice me noticing her? I quickly looked away, pretending to tie my shoelaces, hoping I hadn't seemed too obvious.

Later, I asked Rajeev again. "So she's really shy, huh? Hardly talks to anyone?"

"Yeah," he said with a grin. "Her name's Meera. From what I've heard, she's from a conservative family. She's brilliant, but keeps to herself. Don't get any funny ideas. She's not the type to just chat randomly."

His words only made me more determined. Not in a pushy way, but I wanted to know her, to understand the quiet curiosity that kept pulling me back every day. I promised myself I would find a way to talk to her… somehow.

A few days later, I found myself lingering inside the library, pretending to browse through some reference books I didn't need. Summoning courage, I stepped closer as she paused near the library entrance. "Hi… um, hello," I said, trying to sound casual.

She looked up briefly, startled, and then immediately lowered her gaze. "H-Hello," she whispered, barely audible.

"I… I see you around here a lot. Are you new?" I asked, smiling.

She nodded but didn't look at me. "Yes… first year," she said softly, clutching her books a little tighter.

I tried to continue, "I'm Aditya, by the way. Thought I should—"

Before I could finish, she quickly mumbled, "I… I have to go," and hurried inside the library, leaving me standing there mid-sentence.

I froze for a moment, heart pounding. She hadn't been rude, just shy, almost painfully so. And that made me even more curious. For the first time, someone had caught my attention in a way that made me want to chase, but carefully, patiently.

The next few days, I searched for excuses to pass by the library. I couldn't help it. Every time I caught a glimpse of her, my curiosity and fascination grew.

One afternoon, while practicing with the college cricket team, I spotted her again. She was walking from near the practice nets toward the library, her pace slow, eyes downcast, completely absorbed in her book.

"Hey!" I called out as I jogged toward her, cricket bat still in hand.

She looked up, startled, and froze for a second. I could see the faint pink of embarrassment on her cheeks. "Hi," she whispered, barely audible.

"I was… um, wondering if you like reading in the library often," I said, trying to sound casual. "I mean… you're always there, right?"

She nodded slightly, clutching her book tighter. "Yes… I… like it," she murmured.

"Cool," I said, scratching my head, unsure what to say next. "I'm Aditya, by the way."

"I-I know," she whispered. Her eyes flicked away immediately, back to the ground.

I smiled, trying to make it easier for her. "I see you around, and I thought I should… say hi. That's all."

Her lips quivered into a small, shy smile, and then she quickly turned and walked into the library. Just like that, she escaped from the conversation, leaving me standing there.

That night, lying in bed, I couldn't stop replaying the encounter. The game had changed. Cricket still mattered, studies still mattered, but now, there was someone who quietly captured my attention. And I was ready to learn the rules of this new game.

One afternoon, I noticed her struggling with a stack of books near the library stairs. My heart nudged me forward.

"Hey, do you want a hand with those?" I asked softly, keeping my voice gentle.

She looked up, startled, her fingers clutching the top book as if it were a shield. "Oh… um, no. It's fine," she murmured, shifting the pile awkwardly.

"Are you sure?" I insisted, keeping a safe distance. "I wouldn't mind helping, really."

After a pause, she hesitated, then nodded slightly. I took the bottom books carefully and placed them on the table nearby.

"Thank you," she whispered, eyes darting away.

"No problem," I said, smiling. "And you don't have to say anything back if you don't want to."

She didn't respond, but she didn't run either. That small pause felt like a victory.

She always came to the library at the same time, always chose the same corner. So, I began timing my visits, walking past casually, sometimes greeting her quietly: "Hi" or "Good afternoon." Most times, she would nod or whisper back, and occasionally, she would even manage a tiny smile.

I also discovered she liked a particular section on psychology and literature. One day, I casually picked up a book from that section while passing her table.

"Oh… you like this one too?" I asked, keeping my tone light.

Her eyes widened slightly. "Yes… it's interesting," she said softly, glancing down at the pages.

"Maybe you could tell me a little about it sometime?" I asked, careful not to pressure her.

She looked up quickly, eyes wide. "Oh… yes. It's… um… quite interesting," she replied, her voice barely above a whisper.

I smiled gently. "I was just curious… maybe you could tell me what you like about it? I don't get all of it."

She hesitated, tapping the pen against the paper. "Well… it's about understanding why people act the way they do. And… um… it's… complicated," she said, her words slow, careful.

"Complicated is fine," I said. "I like complicated. Makes it more fun to figure out."

Her lips twitched into a tiny smile, almost imperceptible. That small gesture felt like a victory. "I… I can try to explain a bit," she murmured.

We spent the next fifteen minutes sitting across from each other, talking quietly. I asked simple questions about the book, and she answered, her shyness softening as she spoke about a topic she loved. I didn't interrupt, didn't rush, just listened.

"See you tomorrow?"

She didn't answer, just walked away. I leaned back in my chair, letting out a quiet breath.

The next few days, I tried to find ways to run into her around campus without seeming obvious. I would linger near the cafeteria, pretend to read a book near the library entrance, even choose benches that were on her usual path between classes.

But every time I approached, she seemed to notice me a step ahead, turning a corner, ducking behind a column, vanishing into a crowd. It was like chasing a shadow. Part of me was frustrated, but another part couldn't help but admire her caution.

One evening, I final, saw her inside the library, sitting at her usual corner desk, completely absorbed in her notes. I took a deep breath and walked over.

"Hey… can we talk for a minute?" I asked, trying to keep my voice calm.

She looked up, startled, and instinctively closed her notebook slightly. "What… what is it?" she asked, eyes wary.

"I noticed you avoiding me around campus," I said, sitting down across from her. "Why are you doing that? Did I… do something wrong?"

She bit her lip, then looked away. "No… it's not that you did something wrong. You just… don't get any wrong ideas. I'm not going to be in any sort of relationship, with you or anyone. And if someone saw me talking to a boy… it wouldn't go well with my family."

Her words hit me like a cold wave. I could see the seriousness in her eyes, the fear of crossing boundaries set by her family.

"I… I understand," I said quietly, forcing a smile. "I'm not here to make things complicated for you. I just… I am sorry."

She softened a little at that, nodding. "Thank you for understanding. I appreciate that."

Her words echoed in my mind long after I left the library. I thought she liked it when we spoke the last time in the library. She was clear—no relationships, no distractions, no compromises. At first, I was disappointed. But as the day went on, I realized there was only one thing I could do: respect her wishes and redirect my energy.

The next morning, I stepped onto the nets with a renewed sense of purpose. I pushed all thoughts of her to the side. I didn't check the library, I didn't even look at her when she passed by the practice nets. She walked past me one afternoon, books in hand, and I kept my focus locked on my drills.

Days turned into a routine. Practice, matches, college classes. My World shrank back to my game and my goals. And strangely, the absence of distraction felt liberating. My timing improved, my reflexes sharpened.

Yet, a quiet part of me missed seeing her. Not in the longing way I had before, but as a small reminder that some things in life aren't meant to be rushed. And for the first time in a long while, I felt like I was back in control of my own life.

It was the college semifinal. The ground buzzed with energy. Students lined up along the boundary, some sitting on the steps, others cheering from the shade of the trees. For once, the entire college seemed united, eyes fixed on the game.

I noticed her too, but only briefly. She was standing a little away from the crowd, near the far corner, clutching a notebook against her chest. For a moment, my heart tugged, but I forced myself to look away. Focus, I reminded myself. No distractions.

The game began. Our team needed me, chasing a tricky target with wickets falling quickly. I went in at number four, the pressure heavy on my shoulders. Ball after ball, I reminded myself of the hours in the nets. Footwork, patience, shot selection. The cheers faded, the pressure dulled. It was just me, the ball, and the bat.

A cover drive brought me my fifty. A square cut, perfectly timed, took us to the brink of victory. And when the winning runs came, a lofted shot over mid-on—the roar of the college was deafening. Teammates rushed onto the field, lifting me up, clapping my back, shouting my name.

But somewhere, through the blur of celebration, my eyes searched that corner. She was still there, standing quietly, watching me with an expression I couldn't quite read. Not joy, not just admiration, but something softer, deeper.

After the crowd thinned and the noise settled, I sat on the ground, packing my kit bag, sweat dripping down my neck. That's when I saw her walking toward me. Each step measured, hesitant, as if she was still deciding whether to turn back.

"Congratulations," she said softly, stopping just a step away. "You played really well."

For a moment, I just stared. Her words, though simple, felt heavier than all the cheers I'd received that day. It was the first time she had spoken to me without the wall of distance between us.

"Thank you," I replied, my voice low, almost careful, afraid of breaking the fragile moment.

She looked down at her notebook, clutching it tightly. "I… I watched the whole match. You were… different out there."

I smiled, a small, genuine smile. "Cricket is where I feel most like myself."

For the first time, her lips curved into the faintest smile.

"I realized I was spending too much time alone in the library. And… maybe I could use some company sometimes." Her words were quiet, careful, but there was a spark of courage in them.

"Company, huh? I can do that," I said, feeling a small surge of satisfaction. Second victory of the day.

From that day on, our friendship began to take shape. We would meet occasionally in the library. Slowly, she started opening up, sharing her own thoughts, favorite books, and even her struggles adjusting to college life.

Another afternoon, while sitting under a tree near the college canteen, she confided, "I never thought I'd have someone to talk to like this here… ."

"You don't have to worry about being judged or anything else,' I replied. "I've messed up a lot, believe me. I'm hardly perfect.'

She shook her head. "No, it's not about that.' She said softly, her fingers tracing the edge of her book. "It's just… in my house, even talking to a boy is seen as wrong. My parents have always told me what's good for me, what's not. I grew up… learning to stay silent rather than risk their anger."

She looked up at me then, her eyes glistening, half-defensive, half-relieved.

"I was scared that if anyone saw us together, I'd be blamed… and they will stop my studies. That's why I tried to stay away."

For a moment, I didn't know what to say. All I could manage was, "I'm glad you didn't."

Her lips curved into a shy smile, and in that instant, the distance between us truly began to shrink. And slowly, the boundaries shifted.

One evening, when the library was about to close, I whispered, "Want to… get some tea? Just nearby. I'll drop you back before anyone knows."

She hesitated, clutching her bag tighter. "It's too risky. If someone sees me."

"They won't," I promised. "We'll be careful."

That was the first time she got on my bike. She wore a plain white scarf, wrapping it tight around her face, only her eyes visible. My heart raced as she sat behind me—her hands barely touching the side of the seat, careful not to rest on me.

We stopped at a tiny stall outside campus. She kept her head down, sipping quickly, always alert.

"This is crazy," she murmured, her eyes darting around.

"Maybe," I said, grinning.

She looked at me then, her eyes softening above the scarf. For a second, I swore she wanted to smile, but she quickly looked away.

After that, it became our ritual. A quick ride after classes, always with her scarf, always careful to return before her mother's scooter arrived at the college gate.

Some days, we'd just ride around aimlessly, the city buzzing around us while she sat quietly behind me. I never pushed her to talk. Just knowing she was there was enough.

Weeks passed. Our conversations grew longer, and I noticed her laughing more freely, letting the shyness melt away in moments that felt effortless.

But there was one rule she made me swear by: **no calls, no texts, no written words at all.**

"If you ever message me, even by mistake," she said firmly one evening, "my family will find out. And then it's over… for both of us."

So we never did. We lived in silence outside of those stolen hours.

We walked together in the campus everyday. One day somewhere along the path, our conversation quieted. The air between us seemed charged, familiar yet different, heavier with unspoken words.

She paused near a shaded bench. "I like… I mean, I really enjoy spending time with you," she said, voice soft, almost hesitant.

I stopped too, searching her face. "I… like it too," I admitted. The words felt heavier than I expected, but I couldn't take them back.

There was a long pause, then, almost instinctively, our hands brushed. I froze, and she froze too, a faint blush spreading across her cheeks. I could feel the warmth of her hand where it touched mine, subtle but electric.

"I…" she started, then shook her head slightly, laughing nervously. "I'm awkward sometimes."

"No," I said, my voice steady despite the racing of my heart. "You're… perfect the way you are."

She looked at me, eyes wide, searching for any hint of teasing. Finding none, she smiled—small, shy, but genuine. And then, almost like a decision she had been holding back, she laced her fingers through mine.

The world seemed to shrink around us—no campus, no other students around, just the two of us and the warmth of that first intentional touch. From that moment, the line between friendship and something more blurred. I let myself imagine what it might be like to have her by my side. Not just as a friend, but as my girlfriend. My first love.

We hadn't officially named it yet, but it didn't matter. Every moment we spent together confirmed that we liked each other. The little teasing, the shared secrets, the way she looked at me when she thought I wasn't noticing. It was all a gentle, exhilarating thrill.

For me, this was different from anything I had felt before. She was my first girlfriend, my first real taste of love, and it made my world feel brighter, fuller, and strangely lighter, even with all the pressures of cricket and college around us.

And for the first time, I felt that balance I had longed for. Between my passion, my responsibilities, and the new, tender emotions that were beginning to take over my heart.

CHAPTER 5
BROKEN WINGS

I HAD BEEN planning for the day where I would finally tell her exactly what I felt. My first real confession of love. I asked her to skip all her classes for the morning, promising I'd bring her back before college ended.

"Do you want to watch a movie?" I had asked, trying to make it casual. She smiled and nodded, squeezing my hand softly.

Everything was perfect. We laughed, shared popcorn, and whispered silly comments during the movie. My heart was pounding with excitement and nerves that after this, everything would change.

As the credits rolled, I took a deep breath, ready to tell her how I felt. We walked out of the theater, hands intertwined, stepping into the mall's bright corridors.

But fate intervened. We saw them. Her parents. Standing a few feet away, eyes fixed on us. Time seemed to freeze. My chest tightened. Her grip on my hand faltered.

We froze.

The silence stretched like an eternity. Not a word was spoken. Just the heavy weight of disapproval hanging in the air. Before I could say anything, they gently, firmly, took her by the arm and guided her away.

"Wait—please!" I tried, my voice barely above a whisper. But they didn't turn. She looked back at me, eyes wide and apologetic, before being pulled out of sight. I stood there, heart pounding, words trapped in my throat. All I could do was watch her go, feeling the sharp sting of helplessness.

I started my bike, my mind still replaying the scene at the mall over and over. Her parents. Their silence. The way they had taken her away without a single word. My heart felt heavier than the storm outside.

I called Karan as I navigated the slippery roads. My voice was tense, the words tumbling out in a rush. "Karan… something happened. Her parents saw us… they took her away. I—"

The next moment everything changed. The road was slick, and my mind was elsewhere, caught in a whirlwind of thoughts. The tires lost grip. My bike skidded. I flew. The world spun violently. Pain exploded through my body.

I woke up in the hospital, the sterile white walls a stark contrast to the storm that had been raging outside. My leg throbbed with a sharp, unbearable pain. My shoulder ached terribly, dislocated. Bruises and cuts covered me like a map of the accident.

But above all, my heart sank as I saw the pain in my parents' eyes. Their worry, guilt, and fear reflected back at me, making my own agony feel heavier.

Karan was standing behind my parents. I glanced at him with a concerned look. He understood that I needed to talk to him. Karan quietly pulled up a chair next to my hospital bed. The room felt heavy, filled with the ache of pain and uncertainty.

My parents had stepped out to speak with the doctor, leaving me with Karan.

She had made me swear about no calling, but this wasn't a normal situation. I tried dialing her number anyway, my hands trembling, but it went straight to voicemail. My heart sank further with every unanswered ring. I muttered to Karan, frustration and fear thick in my voice, "Get the details… find out what happened. I need to know." Karan nodded grimly. He promised he would do what he could.

Later, the doctor returned with a solemn expression. "The injuries are severe," he said. "Your leg and shoulder will take months to heal properly. You'll need extensive physiotherapy."

The words hit me like a punch to the gut. My dreams, the countless hours of training, all of it now seemed to vanish into thin air. A wave of helplessness washed over me.

The next day, Karan returned with news about her. His expression was solemn as he told me, "Her house… it's locked. No one has seen her, and she's absent from college too."

I leaned back on the pillows, trying to steady myself. A cold dread crept through me. The thought of her being trapped or forcibly kept away refused to leave my mind. My heart ached with guilt and fear.

Karan placed a hand on my arm. "Don't panic, man. We'll figure this out. But you need to focus on recovering first. Once you're better, we'll handle this together."

I nodded, though inside, despair gnawed at me. Lying there with my broken leg and dislocated shoulder, my lost dreams, and her silence, it all felt suffocating.

The following months passed in a blur of pain, rest, and slow recovery. My parents hovered around me like guardians, fussing over every meal, every movement, every little discomfort. The care was unconditional, but the more they tended to me, the heavier the guilt pressed on my chest. I felt like a burden, a child trapped in a body that refused to cooperate.

Every quiet evening, while lying on the bed with my leg propped up, my thoughts drifted to her. I tried every possible way to reach her—calls, messages, even asking mutual friends—but every attempt ended in a dead end.

One afternoon, a college friend approached me. "I don't know if you've heard… but she's left the college," he said, lowering his voice. "Her family moved out of the city. Nobody really knows where."

The words struck like a cold wind. And yet… in hindsight, I began to understand. She had been right all along. Her warnings, her insistence that nothing could happen between us—it wasn't to hurt me. She had known the reality of her life, of her family, and I… I had been blind with my own feelings.

A bitter truth settled in me: I might have ruined her life, or at least made it infinitely more complicated. The thought twisted inside me, leaving a hollow ache I couldn't shake.

For the first time, I truly grasped what she had meant when she had told me about her limits. Love, desire, even courage sometimes wasn't enough when the world around you had rules you couldn't bend.

I closed my eyes and whispered to the empty room, "I hope… I hope she's safe. And I hope… one day… she forgives me."

CHAPTER 6
HEALING

WEEKS PASSED. I was sitting on the bed, my leg still in a cast, a dull ache pulsing through my shoulder. The room was quiet except for the soft ticking of the wall clock. Mom came in, sitting beside me, her hands folded over her lap. Her eyes, usually full of warmth, now carried a heaviness I hadn't seen before.

'Adi' she began softly, 'do you think we want to see you in pain? That your father suffers every time he sees you hurt?'

I looked down at my hands, unable to meet her gaze.

"You know your father… he's getting older. Soon he'll retire, and your brother has already left the house to start his own family, The responsibility of the family… it falls on you now. You've been chasing cricket for years, but look at yourself. It's not meant for common people like us. Your leg, your shoulder… we can't risk our son's well-being any more. It's time to focus on your studies, get a good job, and give us peace."

Her words sank deep. Every word a heavy stone in my chest. I could feel the truth in them, but it cut like a knife.

In a matter of minutes—no, seconds—I realized the magnitude of what I had lost. My dreams, painstakingly built over years of sweat and sacrifice, were shattered. And the girl I had loved, the one person who had become a part of my every thought, was gone, leaving only memories and unfulfilled longing.

The harsh reality pressed down on me. I had lost two of the most important things in my life in such a short span—my love, and my dream.

I leaned back, letting out a long, heavy sigh. The pain wasn't just physical anymore. It was the ache of knowing that life, cruel and relentless, had moved on without me.

For the first time, I truly understood the weight of responsibility. Everything else had to take a backseat now. My life had changed forever, and I had no choice but to follow the path laid out before me.

The first few days back in the campus felt like walking through quicksand. Every step forward seemed to drag me deeper into the weight of what I had lost. Cricket matches went on without me. Her absence lingered in every corner of the campus. And I was left with my books, my bruises, and the silence of my room.

But slowly, almost reluctantly, I began to shift. At first, studying was just a distraction. A way to numb the ache of afternoons without her scarf fluttering behind me on the bike. But somewhere along the way, the distraction turned into determination. If my dream of cricket had ended, I had to build another. If she was gone, I had to find purpose elsewhere.

I buried myself in textbooks until the world around me faded. My friends were surprised, even shocked. Karan would laugh sometimes and say, *"Who are you and what have you done to my friend Adi?"* But behind the joke, I knew he understood.

It wasn't the life I had dreamed of, but it was the life I had. And I was learning, painfully, to live it.

Still, the nights before exams weren't easy. Sleep came in fragments, haunted by memories of what I had lost. Sometimes, in the silence, I could hear the cheer of the crowd on the college ground. But instead of drowning in those echoes, I pushed harder into my studies. Pain had become fuel.

When exam day finally came, I walked into the hall not with fear, but with a strange determination. Every page I turned, every answer I scribbled down felt like reclaiming a piece of myself. By the last paper, I leaned back in my chair, exhausted, but not broken.

Weeks later, the results arrived. I unfolded the sheet with trembling hands and then froze. I had passed. Not just scraped through, but with marks I hadn't thought possible.

Mom's eyes welled up when she saw it. Dad tried to hide his smile behind the newspaper, but I caught him peeking, his chest swelling with pride. That evening, he placed a hand on my shoulder and said, "Adi, this is just the beginning. I know you can do anything if you put hard work in. You've proven what you can do. Now you should think bigger. MBA, or maybe even the civil services exams. We want to see you settled, respected, making a life where no one can question you."

The words carried weight. They weren't a demand, but they were a vision. A father's dream of seeing his son rise higher than he himself ever could.

For the first time in months, our house felt light, as though the air itself had shifted. To celebrate, Dad suggested a trip to Alibaug. It wasn't anything grand, just a short getaway, but for us it felt like a reset button.

The sea breeze carried away months of suffocating silence. I walked barefoot on the wet sand, the waves washing over my ankles, and felt something loosen inside me. At night, we sat together on the terrace of the guesthouse, eating fish fry and laughing at old stories. Dad a bit drunk on two pegs of whiskey.

Dad spoke again, this time with a faraway look in his eyes. "Adi, life doesn't always go the way we plan. But if you stay disciplined, opportunities will open. Maybe one day we'll see you as an officer, someone people look up to."

I nodded quietly, the sound of the waves filling the silence. His dream wasn't mine, not yet, but for now, I was willing to carry it, if only to see that light of pride in his eyes again.

For a brief moment, I let myself breathe. No exams, no broken dreams, no memories clawing at me. Just the warmth of family, and the fragile peace of knowing I was still moving forward.

Almost a year had passed since the accident. Life had settled into a rhythm— coaching classes, books, and the occasional cricket match watched from afar, not played. The ache of loss was still there, but it no longer consumed every waking moment.

One Saturday night, Karan dragged me and Bharat to a small bar near the outskirts of the city. It was his birthday, and he wasn't about to let either of us get away with just a quiet dinner.

The three of us sat around a high table, bottles of beer clinking against each other. Music pulsed through the dimly lit room, laughter spilling from every corner. For the first time in a long while, I felt… normal.

Karan leaned back in his chair, grinning. "To us!" he shouted over the music, raising his bottle. "Survivors of everything life throws at us"

I laughed, shaking my head. Bharat rolled his eyes but clinked bottles anyway. The foam spilled a little, and we all laughed harder than we should have.

Hours slipped by in stories, jokes, and half-drunken arguments about politics and other stuff. By the time the second round was done, the noise around us seemed to blur, leaving just the three of us in our own bubble.

Bharat, usually the quiet one, finally leaned forward, his tone softer than before. "Adi," he said, "are you… are you alright now?

I took a sip of my beer, letting the fizz settle before answering. For once, the truth didn't sting.

"Yeah," I said, nodding. "I'm fine now. Perfectly fine."

But I noticed the way Bharat avoided my eyes, the heaviness in his voice. I frowned. "What about you? You don't seem alright. Something bothering you?"

Bharat hesitated, his fingers tracing the rim of his glass. Finally, he sighed. "I don't know, man. Engineering… it doesn't feel right anymore. I keep thinking of quitting, maybe finding a full-time job instead. At least I'll be earning, helping at home."

Karan shot him a sharp look, but I spoke before he could. I leaned in, my voice steady. "Don't make the same mistake I did, Bharat. Starting from scratch is way harder than it seems. You'll think it's freedom at first, but later… you'll realize what you gave up."

He looked at me, eyes searching mine for sincerity. I didn't flinch.

"See it through," I continued. "Whatever happens after, you'll at least know you finished what you started. Trust me, it's easier to carry that weight than to live with regret."

Bharat nodded slowly, as if the words were sinking into some hidden place. Karan broke the heavy silence with his usual grin, clapping Bharat on the back. "Don't worry, we'll drag you across the finish line if we have to."

Bharat was still nodding at my words, looking half-relieved and half-troubled, when Karan suddenly leaned forward, slamming his empty bottle on the table like a declaration.

"Alright, gentlemen!" he said, eyes twinkling mischievously. "Enough of this serious crap. Life's not an exam question paper and you don't need to overthink it. Now, listen to me. One of my old classmates is getting married next weekend."

I raised an eyebrow. "So?"

"So… you both are coming with me."

Bharat groaned immediately, waving his hand. "No chance, yaar. Exams are around the corner."

Karan's attention shifted to me. "And you, mister tragic hero… don't even think of saying no. I don't want to go alone. We will we back in few hours. Plus it would be good for you to be around new people"

I smirked, leaning back in my chair. "Sorry, man. Not in the mood for a wedding."

Karan narrowed his eyes, then slapped the table so loudly that a couple at the next table turned to glare at us. "Adi, listen to me carefully. If you refuse, I swear I'll kick you so hard, your leg cast will magically come back just to protect itself."

I burst out laughing despite myself. "You're insane."

"Insane? No, my friend. I am a visionary. I can already see us dressed up, eating free food, judging the bride's relatives, watching girls dressed finely for the wedding, maybe even dancing like idiots. Do you really want to miss that?"

"Honestly… yes."

Karan threw his arms in the air. "That's it. I've had enough of your nonsense. I'm coming over tomorrow with my mom's slipper and knocking sense into you."

Even Bharat cracked a laugh at that.

I shook my head, smiling despite my resistance. "You're unbelievable."

Karan leaned closer, pointing a finger at me. "Unbelievable drunk but effective. Mark my words—you're coming. End of discussion. Now finish your beer before I pour it over your head."

The three of us burst into laughter, the heaviness of earlier conversations dissolving into the easy warmth of friendship.

CHAPTER 7
LOST AND FOUND

BHARAT WAS SPARED, thanks to his exams, but I had no excuse strong enough to escape Karan's persistence. Somewhere deep down, I knew he just wanted me out of the monotonous cycle of classes, home, and library. Maybe he thought I needed a little distraction. Maybe he was right.

On the day of the wedding, we rode together, the cool evening breeze rushing past as Karan hummed Bollywood songs completely out of tune. "Mark my words, Adi," he shouted over the noise of traffic, "tonight, something will change for you."

I laughed. "Change? At a wedding? What do you think is going to happen, Karan? Am I going to elope with the bride?"

"Who knows, bro!" he grinned. "Love stories begin in strange places. And trust me, weddings are breeding grounds for them. Everyone is dressed their best, emotions are high, and you… well, you could use a little heart-thumping drama again."

I rolled my eyes but couldn't stop smiling. Somewhere in my chest, a small flicker of excitement stirred, though I quickly pushed it down.

We arrived at the wedding hall, lights glittering against the evening sky, the sound of dhols and shehnai floating through the air. Karan was already in full swing, waving at people he barely knew and dragging me to dance more than once. The place buzzed with colors. Women in dazzling lehengas heavy with embroidery and jewelry glittering under the chandeliers.

I stood back, quietly scanning the crowd while Karan danced and showed off his sick moves to the people around him.

And then, among the glitter, sequins, and chaos—I saw her.

She wasn't dressed like the others. No heavy makeup, no clinking of ornaments, no artificial glitter to catch attention. Just a soft pastel saree draped with simple grace, her hair left open with the slightest wave. And yet… she was the most beautiful girl in the room.

There was something striking about her simplicity, as though she didn't need anything to announce her presence. She laughed at something her friend said, and the sound carried lightly across the hall, reaching me. It wasn't loud, it wasn't practiced. It was genuine.

For the first time in months, my chest tightened—not with pain, but with something dangerously close to hope.

Karan followed my gaze, noticed the change in my expression, and his lips curled into the widest grin I had seen in days.

"Oh ho…" he muttered under his breath, nudging me with his elbow. "And here I thought I dragged you here for no reason. Looks like the universe had other plans."

I shook my head, trying to snap out of it, but Karan leaned closer, whispering in mock seriousness,

"Adi… this is fate. I haven't this spark in your eyes for a long time. Don't you dare waste it. Tonight, we're not leaving until you talk to her."

I don't know why my eyes kept going back to her. I tried to look away, but my gaze betrayed me. And then it happened—she looked back.

For a brief second, her eyes met mine across the crowd. My heart stuttered, caught completely off guard. She didn't look away immediately, either. She held it, just for a moment, and then turned to the friend beside her, whispering something that made her lips curve into a small smile.

Was she talking about me? Or was my mind playing tricks on me again, filling in the blanks like it always did?

I gripped the glass in my hand tighter, pretending to sip, but my throat was dry as sand. I'd felt this rush before, right before walking out to the crease in an important match, bat in hand, knowing all eyes were on me. Except this time, it was just one pair of eyes, and it was enough to rattle me.

Karan returned, piling food on his plate as though there was a competition. "Why are you standing here like a statue? Bro, it's a wedding, not an exam."

I forced my gaze away from her, leaning closer. "Do you know who she is?"

He followed my line of sight, and the grin spread instantly across his face. "AHA! Finally. The wicket's gone. Mr. 'I'm perfectly fine now' has spotted someone. About time."

"Shut up," I muttered, heat rising to my face. "I'm serious. You think Akash knows her?"

Karan raised an eyebrow, clearly enjoying this. "Of course he does. He's the groom. He knows everybody here. Want me to ask him?"

I hesitated. My heart said yes, my head screamed no. "No, forget it. It's stupid."

"Stupid?" Karan smirked. "My friend, stupid is my style. Besides, what's the point of coming to a wedding if not to flirt with fate a little? If you don't ask, I will."

"Please… keep it casual. Don't make it obvious."

"Relax." He clapped me on the back, nearly making me spill my drink. "Casual is my middle name. Watch and learn."

And just like that, he strutted off toward Akash, full of confidence, leaving me standing there with my heart pounding like a drum. I let my eyes wander back to her. She was laughing with her friend again. I stood there, waiting, heart thumping harder than it should for something this small. Karan finally strutted back, a samosa in one hand, a gulab jamun in the other, grinning like he'd just cracked a top-secret mission.

"Well?" I asked, trying to sound casual but failing miserably.

He took his sweet time, biting into the samosa first. "Mmm… crispy. You should try it."

"Karan!" I hissed. "Did you find out anything?"

He wiped his mouth dramatically, then leaned in as if he was about to reveal a classified document. "So… the intelligence report says—she might be from the bride's side."

I blinked. "Might?"

"Yeah." He nodded seriously, like a professor explaining physics. "See, I asked Akash, 'Who's that girl?' and he said, 'Which one?' So I described her—beautiful, simple saree, smile that melted my friend Adi's brains. Basically poetry, bro. And guess what? He shrugged. SHRUGGED! Can you believe it? On his wedding day, with all the guests, the man doesn't even know half of them."

I stared at him. "So you know nothing?"

"Not nothing," he said, popping the gulab jamun into his mouth.

"She's not from his side. Which leaves the bride's side. Basic elimination. Sherlock-level deduction, my friend."

I sighed, running a hand down my face. "You're useless."

"Useless? Excuse me." He pointed his sticky gulab jamun finger at me. "I risked social embarrassment on the battlefield of wedding banter for you. While you were standing here staring at her like a love-struck cow."

Despite myself, I chuckled. "You're useless and an idiot."

Karan smirked, tossing the empty tissue away. "Maybe. But I'm also your only chance of finding out who she is. So… you want me to go deeper into enemy territory?"

I hesitated, stealing another glance at her. She was still laughing with her friend, completely unaware of the storm brewing inside me.

"…Yes," I said finally. "But for God's sake, be subtle."

Karan saluted me with exaggerated flair. "Subtle is my superpower. Don't worry."

Watching him walk away again, I wasn't sure whether to feel relieved… or terrified. He marched off again, chest puffed like he was about to crack the Da Vinci Code. I watched from a distance, half curious, half dreading what nonsense he'd come back with this time.

First, he cornered an old aunty near the sweet counter. I could see her shaking her head while Karan mimed describing someone, waving his hands around as if he was explaining a cricket strategy. Then aunty gave him a plate of jalebis and walked away. Strike one.

Next, he tried with a random uncle sipping juice. Within two minutes, the uncle had his arm around Karan, laughing loudly, clearly telling him life stories he never asked for. Karan extricated himself, looking mildly traumatized. Strike two.

I buried my face in my hand. *This idiot.*

Finally, he approached a bunch of kids running around with balloons, their sherwanis untucked and faces smeared with ice cream. I saw him crouch down, whisper something, and the kids immediately burst into uncontrollable giggles. One of them even smacked him on the head with a balloon before sprinting away.

He tried again, this time offering a sweet from his plate as a bribe. The smallest one snatched it, stuffed it in his mouth, and shouted, "Bhaiya is asking about that girl!" loud enough for half the guests to turn and stare. Karan shot up, red-faced, pretending to adjust his kurta as if nothing had happened. Strike three.

I groaned. *"This buffoon will get us both killed."*

Karan returned towards me, hair ruffled, pride bruised, carrying a glass of nimbu soda like a defeated warrior.

"Well?" I asked, crossing my arms.

He took a dramatic sip before answering. "The verdict is in, my friend."

"And?"

"She's not related to the bride either."

I blinked. "What?"

"Yep. Not cousin, not classmate, not even one of those distant-relatives-who-appear-only-for-weddings types." He threw his hands up. "She's a ghost, bro. A mystery. Maybe she just walked in for free food. Honestly, respect."

I groaned. "You mean to tell me, after interrogating half the baraat, you've got no clue who she is?"

"Excuse me," Karan said indignantly. "I now know that her uncle isn't a retired colonel, that aunty has diabetes and is still jalebis, and that kids find me devastatingly funny. That's a LOT of intel.'

"You're hopeless," I muttered, shaking my head.

But then, as I stole another glance at her. Her quiet smile, the way she carried herself, so different from the glittering crowd. I couldn't help it. Something about her tugged at me, stronger than reason.

Karan nudged me, catching the look in my eyes. "You're not gonna let this go, are you?"

I stayed silent.

He smirked. "Alright then, Romeo. Don't worry. If she's not from the groom's side, not from the bride's side… then who knows? Maybe fate just brought her here. And if that's the case…" He winked. "…fate's gonna make sure you meet her."

Just as I was beginning to think she might remain a ghost in the crowd, I saw her rise from her seat. My eyes tracked her as she walked gracefully to the stage, where the bride was surrounded by relatives and friends.

They embraced warmly, the bride's face lighting up as if she hadn't seen her in years. That single moment told me everything—I had been wrong. She wasn't a stranger crashing the wedding for free food. She *knew* the bride.

"See? Mystery solved," Karan muttered beside me, munching on a gulab jamun. "She's connected. Now, we just need to find *how*."

But before I could even blink, she was already climbing down the stage with her friend. They didn't linger for the rituals, nor for the dinner. Instead, they made their way directly toward the exit.

"Wait—she's leaving!" I whispered sharply.

Karan dropped his sweet and cursed. "Arre yaar, abhi toh aayi thi!"

We hurried out, weaving through guests, and caught sight of them stepping into a waiting auto-rickshaw. I didn't think twice.

Karan and I bolted to my bike.

The night air hit us as I kick-started it. The auto's taillight flickered faintly ahead, swaying as it moved through the dimly lit road. My heart was pounding, not from the chase, but from the strange desperation building inside me.

"Bhai, we're literally stalking a stranger," Karan shouted over the engine roar, though there was amusement in his tone.

"Shut up and hold on."

Karan leaned forward, whispering in my ear, "Bro, this is starting to look like a Bollywood thriller. Next thing you know, she'll vanish into thin air."

The auto rumbled through the quiet road before stopping abruptly near the entrance of a narrow lane. She and her friend stepped out. She adjusted her scarf before walking ahead, her friend close beside her. The lane was cloaked in darkness, lit only by a weak yellow bulb hanging from a pole.

"Dude, what are you scared of? What's the worst that can happen? She might reject you. Go on," Karan whispered, nudging my shoulder.

I shot him a glare. "No. The worst that can happen is she might scream, we end up in jail, and get our asses kicked by the cops. After that, my dad bails me out just to kick my ass again."

Karan smirked. "Wrong. The real worst thing that could happen is that your dumbass falls in love with her, and she dumps you after a while. Then I'll be stuck babysitting another crying, drunk-ass version of you. Again. Now grow some balls and go talk to her. I'll keep the engine running, just in case."

I let out a shaky breath, muttering, "Why do I even listen to you?"

"Because I'm always right," Karan grinned, revving the bike softly.

I stopped the bike a few steps away from her, parking on the opposite side of the road. My instincts screamed that this wasn't a good idea, but Karan leaned over and gave me a small push. "Go on, Romeo. Time to embarrass yourself."

With legs that felt more like jelly than bone, I began walking toward her. Each step echoed louder in my head than it did on the asphalt.

I could sense her attention turning toward me even before I looked up. When I finally did, her eyes were locked directly on mine. There was no running now.

For a split second, I wanted to turn back, mumble some excuse, and vanish into the shadows. But something held me in place—my ego, maybe, or that invisible pull she seemed to have over me.

Her expression was unreadable, calm yet curious, and it made my chest tighten. I swallowed hard, my words fumbling at the edge of my tongue.

My thoughts started to discourage me. I wish I had never met Karan. All he causes me is trouble. And why the hell do I have to listen to him? And why the hell did I have to turn into a daredevil now?

I've only seen this girl for an hour, and here I am, approaching her like some hero in a cheap Bollywood flick. What am I even going to say? "Hi"? "Nice weather"? Idiot.

But with every step closer, my heart pounded harder, like a drumline inside my chest. And then, everything shifted.

The moment I saw her face clearly, the noise in my head died down. The world itself seemed to grow still, as if time had slowed just for me. God or fate, or whatever cosmic force was out there had pressed pause, giving me a moment to take in His finest creation.

She wasn't just beautiful. She was the definition of beauty. That flawless skin, so radiant it seemed to glow even in the half-darkness of the lane, like moonlight had chosen her as its vessel.

Her eyes… God, those eyes. Hazel, deep, alive. They didn't just look at me—they spoke. They carried stories I ached to listen to. Stories of laughter, of pain, of secrets no one else had been allowed to hear. Even the sad ones, I wanted them all.

Her hair fell like a curtain, trying to veil her eyes, but it failed. With one simple, delicate motion, she tucked the strands behind her ear. It wasn't just a gesture. It was an invitation, a challenge, a silent connection.

And in that instant, I forgot all the stupid reasons to turn back. I forgot Karan, the bike, the fear of being an idiot. All I could think of was her.

Oh god, she's staring at me!

"Hi… can I talk to you?" I blurted, my heart almost crawling up my throat.

"About what?" she asked. Her voice—soft, soothing, like music I'd never heard before, washed over me. She could've been reading out tax laws and I'd still sit there smiling like an idiot.

"Yes. About what." I repeated in my head, grinning like a fool. *What a beautiful selection of words.*

Oh god, she's waiting for me to say something!

I was about to spew gibberish when my phone rang. Nishant. My cousin. A photographer-slash-assistant director for a studio in Mumbai. I didn't pick up, but in that moment I realized something. Sometimes you don't know you need a savior until one calls you.

"Actually…" I stammered, "I'm a photographer. And I think you're really cute. Is there any chance I could get a few clicks of you for my social media?"

Oh god. Did I just say that? That's it. Dumbest pickup line in the history of mankind. Please, earth, open up and swallow me.

Her eyebrows tilted dangerously, like they were preparing for an interrogation.

"You want me to… work with you as a model?" she asked, clearly confused.

"Well, you look like one," I blurted.

That did it. A tiny smile tugged at her lips. She tried to hide it, but too late. I'd already stored it in the forever folder of my memory.

"I don't even know you."

Idiot, Adi! You're supposed to introduce yourself first!

"Right, sorry. My name's Aditya. I saw you at the wedding and… something about you made me want to talk to you. I'm a photographer by profession, and maybe… you could be a help to me."

She paused. Those eyes—hazel, sharp, knowing, studied me like they could see straight into my soul.

"I'll think about it," she said finally, her tone softer.

"Take your time. Should I… give you my number or maybe yours?" I asked, voice trembling with hesitation.

"Give me your phone."

I handed it over like it was the most sacred object in the world. She typed quickly.

"There. That's my Instagram ID. I sent you a request from your account."

"Okay." That's all I managed. Smooth, Adi. Real smooth.

"Goodbye." She started walking away.

I took two steps before it hit me. "Wait. I didn't even get your name!"

She turned, a mischievous glint in her eye. "You never asked."

I stood frozen, internally hearing Karan's voice scream: You dumbass!

Then, with a smirk, she said it. "Radhika."

"Radhika. Nice name. So… goodbye for now."

I turned quickly before I could ruin the moment further. My heart wanted to keep staring at her, but my stupidity had already done enough damage for the night.

Karan was waiting with the bike engine running, smirking like the devil himself. As we sped off, I couldn't resist one last glance back—but she was gone.

What if this was the last time I ever saw her?

"What happened? What did she say? What did you say? She looked angry. Did you screw it up already?" Karan fired questions like a machine gun, grinning ear to ear.

But I stayed quiet. My mind was still trapped in that one moment—the first time I saw her. Strange how you can already feel nostalgic about a memory barely ten minutes old.

Later that night, I finally told Karan what had unfolded.

"She gave me her Instagram ID."

"Great! See? This is why you should always listen to me. So… what exactly did you say to her?"

"I told her I'm a photographer and… that she looked like a model." I puffed up my chest a little, feeling proud.

Karan froze for a second, then burst out laughing so loud I thought the onlookers might complain. "And she fell for that?"

"Obviously," I replied, smug as hell.

"Then she might actually be dumber than you." He kept laughing like a maniac, almost rolling on the roadside, gasping for air, until finally after what felt like ten minutes, he calmed down.

"So," he said, wiping tears from his eyes, "what's your plan now, Picasso? She's probably expecting a photoshoot from the great artist *Aditya the Magnificent.*"

I groaned. "I don't know. I'll think about it."

"Well, think fast." He grinned wickedly. "Because if she messages tomorrow asking for fancy lights, lenses, and an assistant named Ramu, don't come crying to me." And with that, he launched into another round of his irritating, evil laughter.

But he wasn't wrong. I had to come up with something to back up my lie. That was the problem for another day though. For now, I just let his laughter echo in the room, silently praying that Radhika would never call my bluff.

We went to our homes respectively. I was waiting for everyone to sleep so that I could stalk her profile in private. I had been waiting to open Instagram and check out her profile since the moment she sent that follow request in my mobile. But I waited till I was in my room and had time to check out all her beautiful pics. The first thought that came to my mind at her profile was, 'How am I going to compete with her four digits followers with my two digits followers.' Anyways moving forward to the main content. She had posted many pics in different outfits and she looked stunning in each one of them. The one with the traditional dress made my mind wander in future. The urge to message her was getting stronger, but I didn't want to come off too eager.

The thoughts of our meeting didn't let me sleep that night. I didn't want to sleep either. Because if this was a dream, it better be a never ending one. Her face was locked before my eyes even though it had been hours. Her beauty wasn't crafted but simply existed. Her smile, even though it came for a slight moment, lighted up her face. I didn't know where she came from or where she was going. But when my eyes met hers, I felt something for the first time in my life, something shift inside me, like maybe, just maybe, life had brought me to exactly where I was meant to be.

Next day went scrolling through her profile for a millionth time. I didn't leave my phone unattended even for a minute. I couldn't stop staring at the screen, even though I knew it won't make her text any sooner or text me at all. The thought of she ghosting me made me even more impatient. It had only been few hours but it felt like an eternity. Every time the phone buzzed, my heart jumped, only to drop again looking at some random notifications.

Something about her stuck with me. Her smile, maybe her face or the way she spoke. She had a different accent than mine. I kept replaying our conversation in my head. All the things she said and all stupid stuff I said. Maybe she thought I was a fool and might have forgotten about me altogether. I never had such feeling nor I was this desperate for someone's attention, but honestly, I was just hoping that she felt something too, like I did and that I shall hear from her soon.

Two days had passed and no response from her. I had given up hope now. I picked up the phone in anger and almost texted her but stopped at the last moment. I tried distracting myself with everything. Music didn't help. Every song reminded me of how beautiful she was. One song reminded me how she had stranded me on a desert island and left me alone in my sorrows. I tried helping my mom in the kitchen, but it backfired me as I destroyed the meal she was preparing.

That night I was convincing myself that it was nothing. Maybe it was not meant to be. Maybe she was already in a relation. Someone had already stolen the love of my life. And at this point of life, I had gotten accustomed to things not going my way. I reminded myself of the last time when I liked someone and what had followed.

Between all these thoughts, it happened. My phone buzzed. It was her. She had sent me a message.

"Hi." That one 'hi' flipped the whole night around. I read it again and again, grinning like an idiot. My fingers hovered around the screen. Ok, how do I play it cool? Let's start with a decent hello.

"Hello." I replied.

"So is the offer still valid?" she asked. How can I say no to you. You are all that I think about. Okay Adi, play it cool for the next few minutes.

"How about we meet for a coffee and talk about it?" I replied. Way to sound eager Adi. Good job. Great work at playing it cool. I think I should write a book titled – How to lose a girl in one minute.

"Sure." She replied.

"Great." Thank God it worked. "There is one café right around the corner where we met." I suggested.

"Alright." She replied.

"What time shall I be there?" I asked.

"I'll be free after five in the evening." She replied.

"Alright. I'll meet you there at five thirty."

"Sounds good. See you there. Good night" She replied.

The moment the chat ended, I just kept staring at the phone, with an idiotic smile plastered on my face. All that waiting and all that overthinking was worth it. She wanted to meet me. It made me feel like a teenager who just talked to his crush for the first time. It felt like I had scored the winning runs on the last ball of the game.

I was already seated at the café fifteen minutes before the time. She arrived right on time. She was a wearing a red kurti and blue jeans. She looked absolutely stunning in every dress she wore. My heart skipped a beat and my throat lumped when I saw her walk into the café. I forgot how to breathe. Everything around us faded into the background. She wasn't just beautiful, she was stunning. She spotted me and smiled, and that smile melt every bit of the nervousness I'd been carrying since yesterday. I stood up as she approached the table. She sat across from me. I couldn't stop stealing glances. Every detail about her seemed perfect.

"You are looking great." I said, trying to break the ice.

"Thank you." She said with a blushing smile.

"How was your day?" Why is it so hard to talk to someone when you have unconfessed feelings for them.

"Fine." She replied.

"So, how do you know the bride?" I asked her about why she was at the wedding.

"Geeta and I work at the same place." She replied.

"Work? You are not a college student?" I asked.

"What? No. I am here because of my job."

Beauty with brains. Way out of your league Adi – my mind said to me.

"I got transferred here recently. I just moved in the city two months ago. I live in a small rented apartment with five other girls." She said.

"So, where are you from?"

"Goa." She said. That explains the different accent. What a beautiful place to be born and raised in, I thought. We finished our coffee and she suggested we take a walk to her residence.

"How do you know Akash?" she asked me.

"Akash?" I asked a bit confused.

"The groom." She answered.

"Akash. He is a childhood friend of mine. Great guy."

"But Geeta told me that Akash only knows you through your common friend Karan."

For a moment I stood speechless there. I tried to come up with something to defend myself but nothing came out of my mouth. Seeing me struggle for words made her laugh. For the first time I was seeing her laughing from her heart. A smile came across my face by just looking at her.

"So, you tried to know about be?" I asked trying to turn the tables. Her laugh turned into a blushing smile and later into a smirk.

"Well, it's not every day that someone asks you out on the roadside out of nowhere." She replied.

"So, if our last altercation was me asking you out. Does this count as our first date?". She tried to hide her smile from me by looking in other direction.

"We are here." She said, arriving at her the place where she was staying.

"Already."

"Yes. And good bye. I don't want anyone to raise their eyeballs in this neighborhood." She told me and moved towards the gate.

"But you didn't answer my question."

"Good bye." She said firmly. She didn't answer my question. But I found my answer. She did think about me.

That night I was waiting for her message desperately. She finally texted me.

"We never talked about the main topic we were supposed to discuss." She texted.

"What topic?"

"Have you forgotten?"

"No. I mean whenever you are free." I wished she had forgotten about that.

"How about Sunday?" She asked

"Works for me."

"Alright. Just send the time and address. I'll be there." She said.

"Great. It's a date." I replied with a smiley emoji.

"Good night." She replied.

Next morning it was time to call Nishant. He might need some convincing.

"Where are you?", I asked him.

"At home."

"How are you?"

"What?"

"I mean, are you busy or something?"

"Not at the moment. Do you need something?", He asked.

"No, absolutely not. Why would you even say that? Can't an elder brother call to check on his younger brother?"

"Are you drunk early morning?"

"Just shut the fuck up and meet me in an hour." I said angrily. See, this is the problems with guys. You try to give them respect but they think like I need a favor or something.

Two hours later behind college campus.

"There you are. Have a seat. *kaka don cutting dya.*"

"How's work?" I asked Nishant.

"As usual."

"Any new project?"

"No. Just some freelance work and some…"

"Speaking of work. I have some work for you." I interrupted him.

"What kind of work?"

"Photoshoot. See, there is this girl. A friend of mine. She is trying her hand at modelling."

"Model? And your friend?", now he interrupted me. I had to fake a smile to that poor joke.

"I told her that my brother is the best fashion photographer in this city. I'll check if he is available tomorrow as he is always busy" I said with a fakest fake smile.

Nishant was easy to persuade. We finalized a location. A resort with a lake view. A texted her the whereabouts and we decided to meet next day at the location in the afternoon.

I kept glancing at my watch, then at the entrance gate. An auto rickshaw stopped at the resort's entrance. Radhika stepped out with her friend.

She was wearing the most beautiful gown I had ever seen, and for a moment, time seemed to pause. She looked like an angel. She had always looked beautiful in her pictures, but reality was beyond anything I had imagined. My mind struggled to believe she was walking toward me.

"Hi," I said—though no sound came out, only a rush of air.

"Hi."

"You're looking… great."

"Thank you."

"I haven't seen this dress before."

"What?" Her brows knitted in confusion.

"I mean… on your profile. Where you've posted your other pictures," I explained awkwardly.

"So, you've seen all of them? Are you stalking me?"

"More like… admiring," I replied. There it was again, her smile. And the way she tried to hide it made it even more special.

"She's my friend Priya," Radhika said.

"Hi." Priya extended her hand.

"Hi," I replied, giving a small wave, though my eyes stayed fixed on Radhika.

"This is my cousin Nishant. He's also my assistant. Still learning, but I'm helping him." Nishant shot me a quick glare, but I knew he understood. Boys always understand their given assignment without any prior briefing.

We headed toward the lakeside to set up. The water flowed calmly, fringed by lush greenery. And there I was, standing on the shore, looking at the most beautiful girl to ever exist. It felt like a dream.

While Radhika spoke to Priya. Likely asking if she looked alright. I noticed a hint of nervousness in her posture. She smoothed her gown, glanced at me and quickly looked away. Nishant began giving her directions: where to stand, which way to turn, how to angle her gaze. He started clicking photos, and I admired her from behind the camera setup.

Nishant adjusted the tripod while I stood a few steps away, pretending to check the light but really watching her.

"Hold this for me. I mean won't it be better if we use this light reflector from this angle?" Nishant handed me the reflector.

"Good job." I replied.

I moved closer to Radhika, holding the round silver sheet at just the right angle to catch the sunlight on her face.

She squinted at me. “You’re blocking the view.”

“You’re the view.” I spoke under my breath. Maybe she heard me. She turned to her right to hide her smile.

“Turn a bit to the left,” I said, pretending it was purely for the light. She obeyed, and I noticed a loose strand of hair falling across her cheek. Without thinking, I reached forward and stopped in my steps.

She sensed my motivation and froze for a moment, just enough for me to notice. Then she looked away quickly, pretending to fix the drape of her gown.

Nishant was clicking away candidly, completely oblivious, or pretending to be. Boys have that sixth sense.

We moved to a new spot under a large tree where sunlight fell in broken patches through the leaves. I offered my hand to help her step over a root. She took it without hesitation, her grip warm and firm. A current travelled through my vein the moment she touched me. I didn’t want to let her go and for some reason, she didn’t let go either, and I didn’t remind her.

Nishant lined up the next shot. “Alright, one more pose.”

Radhika tilted her face toward the lake. The reflection of light off the water painted her in a soft glow, and I couldn’t stop staring at her.

“I think you have forgotten we came here for work.”

“I am doing my work.”

“Does you work include staring at me?”

“It’s part of the process. Making sure the subject fells appreciated.”

She gave a mock sigh. “So this is your photography technique? Flattery until the camera melts?”

“It works, doesn’t it?” I countered.

She looked away, pretending to examine the lake, but her smile stayed. The water reflected in her eyes, and for a moment I couldn't tell if the light on her face was from the sun or from her.

By the time we finished the last set of shots, the sun had dipped low. Priya and Nishant were packing up the equipment, leaving me and Radhika by the water.

She slipped off her heels and stepped onto the cool grass, letting the hem of her gown graze the ground. "Feels good to just… stop for a minute," she said, looking at the horizon.

"Yeah," I replied, watching the reflection of the sky ripple in the water. "Feels like the kind of view you don't want to ruin with too many words."

She smiled faintly. "And yet, here you are."

"Fair," I admitted, chuckling.

"But… I don't know. We've been around each other all afternoon, and I still don't know much about you. Except that you look good in every frame."

"Why do you want to know more? What if we never meet again?" she said, glancing at me.

I hesitated. The question felt heavier than her tone suggested. I couldn't process the thought of not meeting her again.

"Then I'll have still met you at least this one time," I said quietly. "The sun is not set yet and maybe I'll remember this afternoon a lot longer than I expect to. Maybe forever."

Her gaze changed. "Alright. Ask me something?" She said maybe just out curiosity.

I thought for a second. "What's one thing people usually get wrong about you?"

She tilted her head, considering. "That I'm always confident. I'm not. I just… pretend well."

"I get that. Like you were pretending when you arrived here before. You looked a bit nervous. Same with photography, half the time I'm just hoping I don't mess up the shot." I said trying to act smart.

"So, you're telling me my photographer today was faking it?"

"Not faking," I corrected. "Just… figuring it out as I went."

She looked at me then, her voice softer. "And what have you figured out so far?"

"That I like this part," I said, gesturing at the space between us. "The part where we stop being strangers."

Nishant's ringtone broke the quiet. His hands were full packing up the setup. He picked up the call and put it on speaker mode. It was my mother (his aunt) calling.

"Where are you? I want to talk to your mother." She asked.

"I just finished the shoot near the lake. Will be home in an hour. Adi is with me." Nishant replied. My head snapped toward him.

"Nishant!" I whispered.

"Adi is with you? What is he doing with you. Did you need a helper? I have never seen him hold a camera." Mom making sure that I stay single.

"Cut the damn call." I begged Nishant.

"He can't even click decent pics with his mobile." Mom still continuing her rampage. Nishant finally dropped everything and picked up the phone and ran in the distance.

Radhika turned to me slowly, her lips twitching. 'So, you've been lying to me the whole time?' It was the first time I saw anger on her face.

"Okay, yes, technically… I'm not a photographer. And I am sorry about that. I didn't want to lie to you. But when I approached you the first day we met, I… didn't know what to say. I had seen you for the first time and I couldn't bear the thought of never getting to know you. So, I came up with the photographer story. Not to fool you. Just to have a reason to keep talking to you." I tried to save my sinking boat.

Her eyes softened just a fraction, though her lips stayed pressed together.

"I may not be the guy behind the camera, but I've been watching you all day. And not one moment of it has been fake."

She let out a breath, half a sigh, half a laugh. "You're ridiculous."

"I am being ridiculously honest and trust me it was not easy speaking my heart out."

A faint blush crept onto her cheeks, betraying her attempt to stay annoyed. She turned toward the others. "You're lucky you can talk your way out of things."

Nishant was back after hanging up the call and almost ending my love story before it even began. "We are ready to go."

Radhika slipped her heels back on, giving me one last smile before heading toward the others.

"Where does this leave us?"

"Guess we're not strangers anymore," she said over her shoulder.

"No,' I murmured to myself. Not anymore."

We reached the resort entrance. Priya was already checking her phone for a ride back.

"Auto is on the way," she announced.

Radhika stood a little apart, arms folded loosely, looking down the quiet road. I wanted to say something clever, something that would keep the moment alive, but all I could think of was how quickly the day had gone.

"I wish this day never ended."

She glanced at me with a small smile. "I think we've had enough surprises for one day."

I chuckled. "You still mad?"

She tilted her head. "A little." Then, with the faintest blush, she added, "But… I've decided to forgive you."

The auto arrived sooner than I expected. Priya slid inside first. Radhika lingered by the open door, looking at me.

"You know," she said, "next time you want to talk to someone… maybe just say hello. No need for fake résumés."

I smiled. "So… there's a next time?"

She bit her lip to hide her smile and stepped into the auto. "Bye," she said, just loud enough for me to hear.

"Bye," I replied, watching as the rickshaw rattled away down the dimly lit road, carrying her away from me.

Nishant came up beside me. "Well," he said, smirking, "at least she didn't throw her shoe at you."

I kept my eyes on the fading taillights.

We started the bike and began our journey back to our homes. I dropped Nishant at his place and we decided to meet in the morning. It was past 11:30 when my phone lit up.

Radhika: So… do you always lie to girls you meet for the first time?

I smiled at the screen, imagining her curled up somewhere, maybe in bed, hair untied, that tiny crease in her forehead when she's half-serious.

Me: Only the really pretty ones.

Radhika: Smooth. Doesn't work on me.

Me: Worked enough for you to text me this late.

There was a pause. I pictured her reading that, pretending to be unimpressed, but smiling anyway.

Radhika: I Still think you are not even good at assisting the photographer.

Me: That's fair. But I was an excellent admirer.

Radhika: You mean stalker.

Me: Romantic observer.

I could almost hear her laugh through the dots appearing and disappearing on the chat.

Her next message came with a smiley.

Radhika: Goodnight

Me: Goodnight

I stared at her "last seen" for a while, realizing I was smiling at my phone like an idiot.

CHAPTER 8
EUPHORIA

THE NEXT MORNING after the shoot, I met the boys at our usual spot. Nishant was leaning against the counter, sipping his cutting chai like he'd been waiting hours to roast me. Karan sat on a stool, stirring his cup slowly, his smirk already unbearable.

"Bhai," Karan started, "I still can't believe you looked her straight in the eye that day and said – Hi. I'm a photographer." He said putting on a mocking serious face.

Nishant chuckled. "And the best part? You weren't even holding the camera. I was!"

I groaned. "You guys act like I had time to come up with something better. She was right there… looking like that."

Nishant slapped the table. "So your brain just defaulted to 'Hi, I'm a guy with a DSLR'"?

"You were there, man. You didn't stop me." I pointed at Karan.

Karan grinned. "Why would I stop you? I was the one who pushed you towards her. This was pure entertainment. You think I'd interrupt such art in motion?"

"kaka ajun ek cutting dya." I asked for another cup of tea

I took a sip, letting the heat wake me up. "Anyway, it worked, didn't it? We talked. We connected."

Nishant raised an eyebrow. "Until my phone rang and revealed everything."

"I can't believe my own mother thinks so little of me." I said.

"Her face, man. She went from "aww, cute photographer guy" to "I'm gonna drown you in this lake." Nishant said and Karan laughed so hard he nearly spilled his tea.

"She was angry," I admitted, "but then I made her smile with my charm."

Nishant smirked. "Let's just say you got away luckily."

"Whatever. Point is, I don't want this to end. I'm going to see her again."

Karan leaned back, crossing his arms. "And what's the plan this time? Magically become a chef? A wildlife expert?"

I grinned. "No lies. Just me."

Karan tapped his cup against mine. "Good. But we are still coming. Someone has to witness the sequel."

I didn't say it out loud, but as the steam from the chai curled into the air, I was already picturing her smile again. I texted her immediately.

Me: Hi. Just wanted to let you know the pics are ready.

Radhika: Fine. I'll send you my email id. Send me via mail.

"What did she say?" Karan asked.

"She wants me to send the pics through email." I replied. And they started laughing again. My phone buzzed again.

Radhika: Just kidding. Can we meet in the evening?

Me: Six thirty. Same café?

Radhika: See you there. Bye.

When I arrived, she was already there, sitting by the window, sunlight spilling across her hair like it had personally decided to highlight her. She waved, and for a second I forgot how walking worked.

"You're on time." she said.

"Trying to do better."

I sat down, pulling out my phone. "Ready to see your pictures?"

She nodded, leaning closer as I swiped through them, each frame showing her in different poses, hair catching the light, the lake's calm water behind her. She grabbed my hand and took it close to her see the photos from a better view. My heart started racing rapidly. What if my hand starts sweating and she finds it disgusting?

"They're… nice." she said, biting back a smile.

"Nice?" I pretended to be offended. "That's all?"

"Well, considering you didn't actually click them" Her voice trailed off into a smile.

I laughed, shaking my head. "I knew you'd bring that up."

That's when I saw them. Outside the café window. These guys have no boundaries. Karan and Nishant, sitting at a table across the street, sipping chai like they were international spies staking out a target. Karan had sunglasses on, at 7 p.m.

Radhika followed my gaze. "Do you… know those two guys staring at us?"

I coughed. "Uh… no. Total strangers."

We finished looking through the pictures, and I couldn't help trying to keep her a little longer. We ordered coffee, drifted into talking about travel, music, and some gossip from her office. Every now and then, I caught movement outside. My so-called idiotic friends whispering to each other and making random movements.

Time flew as we spoke. It didn't feel like it we had just met each other a few days ago. It felt like I have known her since forever.

"It's dark already. I should get back to the apartment."

"I'll walk you there."

We left the café and at the exit, the two idiots were still sitting there trying to hide their faces. We were about to pass them when Radhika recognized.

"Hi Nishant." And then she turned to me. "You know… you could've just told me if your friends wanted to meet me."

I smiled awkwardly. "I didn't know these two were gonna be here. You have already met Nishant. And this is Karan."

"Oh, so you are Karan. Akash's friend."

"Yes, and Adi's best friend." Karan replied.

"Anyways it's getting late. See you later. Bye." Radhika sent those idiots off and we started walking towards her apartment.

"You haven't told me why do you stay in such a small apartment."

"What option do I have. I don't know many people here. I have a cousin sister in the city. But she lives with her in-laws in a small home. I stayed with her for few days, but didn't want to be burden on her. The flat we stay is rented by the company. So, the employees like me, who come here from distant places, stay here with each other." Radhika explained me.

I felt sad and angry at the same time. Princess like her deserved nothing less than a Castle to live in. And I promised myself that I will be the Knight in shining armor, who will rescue the princess in distress.

"And what about food?"

"Lunch at office cafeteria. There is a daily tiffin service in this area. Dinner comes from that place." A little distress in her voice. I could sense she was missing home.

"Do you miss home?" I asked. Her expressions changed. Maybe something was bothering her. I felt that I shouldn't have asked her that.

"That's enough questions for a day. And we are here." We had reached the place where we first met.

"Shall I go?"

"Do you have to?"

"Good bye." Whenever she felt shy, she tried to get away from me.

'Wait."

"Go home now." She said trying to escape from me.

"What if there is an emergency." I tried to continue the conversation.

"What kind of emergency?" She asked curiously.

"It could be of any sorts. Maybe I am lost in an unknown place and the only way I could be saved is if I could talk to someone, maybe someone who is not a stranger anymore."

"You are really bad at this. Give me your phone." She said while laughing on my poor attempt. She dialed her contact no. in my phone. "Here"

"The phone is asking for a contact name."

"Umm. How about – Not a stranger.?" She suggested

"How about – Someone Special.?" I replied

"Good bye." She turned her back and went inside without looking at me.

If this was a Bollywood movie, it would be a perfect time for a song playing in the background, portraying my feelings and the excitement of falling in love.

Back at home I was getting restless. I looked at the contact saved in my phone like I have found some lost artifact. Actually, it was way too precious for me. Probably more than any tressure. I was torn between whether to call her or not. I started speaking to myself.

"Should I call her. Too soon. Definitely too soon. But she gave her number so that we could talk. I should wait for at least twenty four hours. But what if I wait too long? Then it'll be weird."

I unlocked the phone, locked it again. Put it in my pocket. Took it out.

Finally, I made up my mind. I took out my phone, opened her contact and just stared at the little call icon, as if pressing it might trigger a nuclear attack. Locked my phone. Threw in on the bed. This process was repeated multiple times. On the fourth attempt my thumb was this close to touching it when my screen lit up.

Incoming Call - Radhika

For a second, I thought I was imagining it. But this was not my imagination, it was her call.

"Hello?" I answered, trying to sound casual.

Her voice came through, playful. "Wow, didn't expect you to pick up so quickly. You were trying to call me right? Were you just staring at my name? How long were you doing this exercise?"

How did she know. Was I that predictable? "No. Absolutely not. Please. I am a very busy guy with busy life. I was about to call someone else about some work that had to be done." I couldn't help being embarrassed and my words made it even worse.

"Uh-huh. You were staring, and now you blushing." she interrupted, laughing softly.

"Why would I blush?" I replied, though I was blushing and it was recognizable from the way I was speaking.

"Just admit it that I am right." She was still laughing at my condition.

"Alright. I admit. I was trying to call to. But couldn't decide." I finally gave up.

"I wish I was there to see your face right now."

"I wish that too. That you were here." I replied. And that changed the tone of the conversation. She didn't talk for few seconds. I imagined here laugh turning into a blushing smile.

"Anyway. just wanted to say thanks again. And I'm not great at waiting."

"Good for me. That saves me from a lot of overthinking."

"You don't have to think before calling me." She replied. Her words eased my mind.

We talked for another ten minutes. As the conversation began to fade, it reminded me of something she had said earlier.

I asked her, "You've been in the city for how long now?"

"Barely two months," she said. "Why?"

"I was thinking maybe I could show you around. A proper welcome tour. You know, local food, famous spots."

There was a small beat of silence before she replied, her tone lighter. "Tempting. But what about your busy schedule?"

"I'll manage."

"Umm okay. But when?"

"Whenever you're free," I said.

She chuckled. "Alright, you've got yourself a date. Deal I meant deal." She tried to correct herself. But I got the answer I needed.

When the call ended, I found myself already thinking about where to take her and planning the whole day with her.

Finally, the day of our first official date was here. I was about to spend the entire day with Radhika. Last night it had rained heavily. Why did the rain always had to play spoil sport.

The mornings in Nashik always looked beautiful. The faint mist that still clung to the river Godavari felt like riding through clouds. I parked my bike outside her lane with helmet in one hand.

She appeared, hair tied in a loose braid, wearing a casual white kurti and jeans. Simple. But it was the kind of simple that made you forget your own name for a moment.

"Is this your bike?" she asked, glancing at the bike.

"No. Neighbors. They let me use it once in a while." I grinned.

"Very Funny." She said in a mocking tone.

I handed her the spare helmet. "Don't worry, I haven't dropped anyone… this year."

She rolled her eyes but smiled anyway, strapping the helmet on.

The engine started and thus starting one of the best day of my life. We went weaving past fruit juice carts, people going for their morning walks, boys playing on the open grounds. She sat a little stiff at first, keeping a polite distance, but somewhere between the first turn and the second, I felt her hands rest lightly on the sides of my jacket.

Our first stop was at near Panchavati. The place had been there for decades.

"This is my go-to breakfast place."

"Great. What are we having."

"Nashik's very own – Missal pav."

"Oo… I always wanted to taste it."

"Don't tell me you haven't had missal pav after two months staying in Nashik. You don't even have to eat here. Try any place in the city and you will get the best Missal you ever had in your life."

"Who was I suppose go with? I didn't have a better company before."

"Fair enough."

"I think I am done eating for the day." She said after finishing her meal.

"Did you like it." I asked.

"Best one I've ever had." she admitted.

"Told you," I said. "Proper Nashik tour."

I ordered two cutting chai and bun maska. She raised her eyebrows.

"What?" I asked.

"Nothing." She answered.

"We finished our breakfast and refreshments and started our journey ahead. We stopped at the old temple on our way to Someshwar. The scent of fresh flowers from a nearby garland shop drifting in the air. She took a garland, incense and some flowers from the shop. We walked barefoot on the cool stone. She looked around and I couldn't stop staring at her. I rang the brass bell that echoed into the riverbanks, and stood in quiet for a moment. She closed her eyes in silent prayer. I didn't ask what she wished for but I wished that all her dreams come true. I wished for her presence in my life till my last breath.

As we rode towards Someshwar, the noise of the city became distant and the sound of wind and constant hum of the engine took its place. Her voice came softer now, almost carried away by the breeze.

"This feels… nice," she said. "Like the kind of day you don't want to end."

I smiled to myself, keeping my eyes on the road. "We'll make it last a bit longer then."

By afternoon, we'd climbed up to Pandav Leni caves, the wind carrying the scent of wild grass. From the ledge, a part of a city could be seen. Vineyards glinting in the distance, the river carving its way through fields, the horizon stretching into soft blue hills. I suggested that we should eat something but she declined because she was still full from the breakfast.

We travelled to the last location of the day at Gangapur Dam, sitting on the low wall as the water caught the orange glow of sunset.

"You seem sad. I thought we were having fun."

"I am. This view just reminded me of something."

"Your home." She didn't reply. But her eyes became moist.

"I am sorry I didn't mean to upset you."

'You didn't upset me. In fact, I haven't laughed this much in my entire life before meeting you."

"Do you miss your home?"

"It's just me and my mother back home. I was ten years old, when we lost my dad. He worked in electricity department. He was bed ridden for more than a year. We lost most of our savings trying to save him. My mother was offered a job after his death, but she declined. She didn't want to leave her only daughter alone at home while she stayed away working. She always said – 'The world can be very cruel.' Since then, we lived off a little pension which we got. Yet she managed to raise her daughter alone. Providing her proper care, education and everything that I will ever need to survive in this world. When I completed my studies, I took the first job which came my way. I can't give my mother her youth back. But I want to make sure she doesn't have to struggle for anything in life anymore.'

Tears started to fall from her eyes. My heart became heavy after hearing her story. I wanted to make all her problems disappear. I decided in that moment to never break her heart. She saw my face turning sad and wiped her tears.

"I am sorry." She said. "I didn't want our day to end like this."

"No no. It's fine. I am glad that to shared your story with me. I am sorry you had to go through such hard times."

We kept our silence for a little while. She kept staring at the setting sun.

"But that doesn't explain why are you here in Nashik."

"I don't think you want to hear the next part." She said smiling.

"Let me guess. Bad break-up." I said. Her face now turned from sad to guilt.

"His name is Rohan. We.."

"I don't need the details." I interrupted her. She sensed that talking about her ex made me uncomfortable.

"Enough about me. Tell me your story." She said, trying to change the mood.

I kept calm for a while. She kept staring at me with curiousness. I hesitated, then told her about my last relationship.

"I liked a girl once," I began, my voice quieter than before. "Few years ago. We went to the same college. I thought I had found the one. The kind of person you start picturing your whole future with." I let out a breath.

"But fate had other plans. The worst part is that we never broke up. One day, her parents saw us coming out of a movie together.

They didn't shout. They didn't even ask questions. They just… took her away. From that day, she vanished. She left her studies. They left their house and moved somewhere, I don't even know where." I picked up a pebble and tossed it into the water, watching the ripples spread.

"That's… rough," she said gently

"You know. I always wanted to be a Cricketer."

Her head tilted. "Seriously?"

"More than seriously," I said, looking at her with a mix of pride and regret. "It wasn't just a hobby. It was… everything. I played for my school team, then the college team, District team, University team. Next step was the State's team."

"Then why did you stop?" She asked curiously.

"The day when her parents caught us, I was coming back home. Alone on my bike. Not the one we came on. It had rained, the road was slippery. My bike skidded, and I went flying. Maybe my head had lot of thoughts going on which resulted in the accident."

Her eyebrows drew together, concern flashing in her eyes.

"I woke up in the hospital with a broken leg, a dislocated shoulder and bruises all over my body. After I gained consciousness, I saw the pain in my parent's eyes.

The doctor said I'd be fine, but the recovery took months. I lost two things that day. One of them was my dream. I saw my old parents taking care of me like I was a new born child. So, I decided to not be a pain in the ass for my parents anymore. Gave up cricket, took studies seriously, completed my bachelor's degree last year and now I am preparing for MBA.'

"I am sorry." She said with tears forming in her eyes.

"It's strange," she said, watching the ripples. "How you can feel like you've known someone longer than you actually have."

"Yeah," I said, looking at her. "Strange in a good way."

"And Maybe," she added after a pause, her voice steadier now, "maybe life also sent you to the right place, at the right time."

A smile tugged at my lips. "Maybe it did."

When we finally got up to leave, I walked her to where my bike was parked. As she climbed on behind me. The ride back was quieter than the morning, but not in a bad way. It was the kind of quiet where words weren't necessary.

When we reached near her lane, she hopped off and stood there for a moment, her hand resting lightly on the seat. "Thank you for a wonderful tour."

"We haven't even covered half of the Nashik."

"Let's save that for another day. And I'm glad we talked today," she said softly.

"Me too," I replied.

"So good bye then." She said half- heartedly.

I nodded, my heart pounding far too loudly for the quiet around us. She turned, about to walk away, and the words slipped out before I could stop them.

"Radhika…"

She paused, looking back at me, expectant. My throat tightened. For a second, I saw it—me telling her everything, how I wanted her to be with me all the time. I wanted to confess my feelings for her. I wanted to tell her that she made me happiest I have ever felt. But the weight of the moment pressed down, and courage betrayed me.

I forced a weak smile instead. "Nothing… just… take care."

Her eyes lingered on mine, searching for the unsaid. And somehow, I knew she had understood.

"Goodnight," she whispered, and walked away.

I watched her walk away, her figure disappearing in the building, and for the first time in a long while, I didn't feel the weight of what I'd lost, but the quiet happiness of what I might have just found.

I started the bike, rode through the quiet streets, and by the time I reached home, my phone buzzed. A message. Her name lit up the screen.

Radhika: Stop thinking so much. Just live this beautiful moment for what it is.

I stared at the words. It felt as though she had read my mind, as if she knew exactly the storm inside me.

The next few weeks passed in a blur, yet every moment with her seemed to stretch into something worth remembering. Our calls, once tentative and short, grew into hours-long conversations that carried us from late nights into early mornings. She would call me the moment she left her office, and I would wait for her call as though it was the most important part of my day. We talked about everything—work stress, small victories, childhood memories or her complaining about the apartment. And every time she laughed, I found myself wanting to say things I still didn't have the courage to.

Lunch breaks slowly turned into lunch dates. Sometimes at a small café tucked in a busy lane, vada-pav at the roadside and sometimes near her office. And every time I saw her, I caught myself thinking the same thing—*how does she look even more beautiful each time we meet?* It wasn't just the way she dressed, or her smile. It was the ease with which she had begun to fit into my days.

On weekends, there were more bike rides. Radhika sitting behind me, her scarf fluttering, her voice cutting through the air as she pointed at random corners of the city—'Stop here!'—to click pictures or taste something from a street vendor. We rode without destinations sometimes, just circling around streets, stopping for chai or to watch the city lights from the riverbanks. Nashik felt different with her, the city that I thought I knew was suddenly new again.

She always mentioned how cramped and inconvenient her current place was, I found myself looking for something better. I told myself it was just to help her settle, but the truth was simpler. I wanted her to live better, to feel like this city could be hers.

When I finally showed her the apartment I thought was perfect—bright, airy, close to her workplace, her eyes lit up. A week later, she and her friends moved in. Karan and I all pitched in on moving day, hauling boxes, setting up furniture, running errands. She laughed at our clumsy teamwork, but every time her eyes found mine, I saw gratitude she didn't put into words.

This wasn't just about helping her move. It was my way of saying, *I care about your world. I want to see you comfortable. I want you to feel at home here—even when you're far away from home.*

A few days later, I found myself outside her new place. Laughter drifted down from the roof, echoing with the sounds of celebration. I looked up and saw fairy lights strung along the railing.

"Hey!" Radhika's voice rang out from above. She leaned over, waving. "Come up!"

I shook my head quickly, forcing a smile. "I'll wait down here."

She tilted her head, amused. "What? Don't be boring. Come on."

"I'm fine here," I insisted.

Her brows knitted together, playful but stubborn. "Once more—come up!"

I raised both hands in surrender. "I can't. Rooftops and I… we don't get along."

For a moment she looked surprised, then her smile softened. She disappeared from view, and before I knew it, she was at the front door, tugging at my arm.

"What's this excuse?" she asked, half-laughing, half-serious.

"I'm afraid of heights," I admitted quietly, embarrassed. "Always have been. Feels like the ground pulls at me."

Her expression changed. "It's okay," she said gently. "You'll be with me. Nothing will happen."

Something in her tone, calm and assuring made me nod. So, I followed her upstairs.

When we finally stepped onto the roof, the cool night air brushed against my skin, and the laughter of her friends filled the space. My chest tightened, but then I felt her hand slip into mine.

Warm. Steady. Certain.

We stood there, fingers entwined longer than either of us intended. At first, it was comfort. Then it became a quiet promise neither of us had put into words yet.

She didn't let go, and neither did I.

In that simple moment, under the stars and fairy lights, trust was born not out of grand gestures, but out of fear shared and comfort offered.

CHAPTER 9
CONFESSION

ONE SUNDAY AFTERNOON we were having coffee at our usual café. Radhika excused herself to the restroom, leaving her phone face-up on the table.

The screen lit up with a buzz. Instinctively, my eyes flicked to it.

A new message.

Ravi: "Sorry for the embarrassing moment. But still had a great time."

My chest tightened. The name stuck. Ravi?

When she returned, brushing her hair behind her ear as she sat down, I tried to sound casual. "So… who's Ravi?"

Her brow creased. "Ravi?"

"Yeah," I said, keeping my tone light, though my fingers tapped the table. "He seems… embarrassed. Why?"

A hint of surprise crossed her face before she chuckled softly. "Oh god. That." She leaned back, sighing. "He's my colleague. He asked me out for coffee last week. I thought it was just a work thing… but apparently, he didn't."

I raised my eyebrows. "So, what happened?"

"He tried asking me out properly," she said, her tone steady but a faint pink rising in her cheeks. "I told him no. Politely."

I exhaled, a tension I didn't realize I was holding easing from my shoulders. "And the 'embarrassing moment' part?"

Her smile curved. "That was him… realizing he'd completely misread me."

She tilted her head, her eyes glinting as if she had caught me red-handed. "Are you jealous?"

"Should I be?"

Her lips curved into a knowing smile, but she didn't answer directly. Instead, she toyed with the glass and said softly, "Let's just say… I had no reason to say yes to him. Because I already like…' She stopped mid-sentence.

For a moment, I froze, the unsaid words echoing louder than anything spoken. I watched her as she sipped her coffee, her smile more genuine now, eyes softer than before.

As the days passed, we grew closer. It was Radhika's birthday. I had spent the past week planning every little detail with the boys. The restaurant had a warm glow that night. Golden lights hanging overhead, soft music playing in the background. It wasn't the fanciest place in the city, but it had charm, the kind of cozy atmosphere that felt just right for her. I picked her up from her place.

When Radhika and I walked in, her eyes widened. Lights, balloons, a simple cake on the table, and all the faces smiling at her. It wasn't extravagant, but it was heartfelt. She covered her mouth with her hand, laughing in surprise.

"You… did all this?" she asked, looking at me.

"Team effort. But yeah, maybe a little bit me."

Her roommates hugged her, the boys cheered, and for the first time, she met Bharat properly.

As the evening carried on, there was cake, clapping, and a few silly dance moves courtesy of the boys. Music played softly in the background, people chatted, and laughter filled the room. Her eyes brighter than the candles that had just been blown out. The room filled with voices and laughter, but my focus never shifted from her. The way she smiled, the way she glanced at me now and then as if silently saying *thank you* without words—it was worth every ounce of effort.

Later, she walked toward me with that mischievous half-smile she carried whenever she was about to say something unexpected.

"You're just standing here, not dancing, not even talking," she said. "You're supposed to be hosting."

"I'm observing," I replied.

"Observing what?" she tilted her head.

"You," I admitted.

She blinked, her lips parting just slightly before she broke into a laugh. "Smooth."

For a moment, her smile softened, her eyes holding mine longer than usual. Then she lowered her voice. "Can we leave?"

I frowned, confused. "Leave? The party isn't over yet."

"I know," she said, brushing a strand of hair from her face. "But I don't feel like being around everyone right now. I want to… just go on a ride. With you."

For a moment, I just stared at her. The music, the laughter, all of it blurred out. She wasn't asking for a grand gesture. Just me and her. Somehow, that meant more than the entire party I'd planned.

"Okay," I said finally, my lips curling into a smile. "Let's go."

We slipped out into the night, the party still alive behind us, but the real celebration just beginning. The night outside was cooler than I expected, the streets quieter now that most of the city was winding down. The faint hum of my bike filled the silence as Radhika slid onto the seat behind me.

Nashik at night had its own kind of beauty. The street lamps casting warm pools of light, the distant glow from temples, and the scent of night-blooming jasmine mixing with the cool air.

For a while, neither of us spoke. She rested lightly, her hands brushing my shoulders, and I could feel her presence in the quietness, steady and unhurried.

"You know… tonight was nice."

"Nice?" I teased. "Just nice? I worked hard on keeping it a secret."

She chuckled, the sound carrying softly in the night air. "Okay, more than nice. It felt… special. Because you were there. All I need is you to be with me."

Her words lingered in my chest longer than I wanted to admit. I kept my eyes on the road, but inside, I was smiling like a fool.

The road curved toward the river, and the bridge stretched out in front of us, lit by the soft yellow of streetlamps. The water below shimmered silver under the moonlight, calm but endless.

She leaned forward a little, her chin almost brushing my shoulder. "Can we stop here?" I slowed the bike and finally stopped midway, drawn by the quiet beauty of the place.

Radhika slid off first, her hair fluttering gently in the breeze. She walked to the railing, her eyes fixed on the river, the lights reflected like broken stars dancing on the water's surface.

"This view…" she said softly, "…it feels like the whole city is holding its breath."

I got off the bike too but stayed a little back, leaning on the handle. The height made my stomach tighten, as it always did. She turned, her hair catching the glow of the lamp above us, and stretched out her hand toward me.

"Come here."

I hesitated, forcing a smile. "You know…"

"I know," she said, stopping me mid-sentence, her voice steady, reassuring. "But you're not alone. Trust me"

Something in the way she said it, calm and certain, pulled me forward. I stepped forward, hesitantly at first, until her fingers wrapped around mine. Warm. Steady. Pulling me closer. The night air pressed against us, carrying the smell of the river, the faint sound of crickets, and the heartbeat I felt in my palm—hers or mine, I couldn't tell.

We stood together at the railing, her hand still holding mine. I dared to look at her. The way her hair caught the light. The way her eyes softened as they found mine.

"See?" she whispered, smiling just a little. "Not so scary when you're holding on."

And then, without warning, the space between us disappeared. The world seemed to still at that moment. The hum of the city, the ripple of the river, even my own fear faded, until there was only her. Our lips met, gently at first, tentative, like two souls finding courage in each other. Then, slowly, the kiss deepened, carrying all the unspoken words we hadn't dared to say. The world fell away. No city, no river, no noise—just the warmth of her lips, the way she leaned into me, and the realization that this wasn't just a moment. This was the moment.

When we finally parted, she rested her forehead against mine. Neither of us said the word, but it hung unspoken between us, stronger than anything either of us could deny.

I laughed softly, my breath shaky. "You're right. Not so scary anymore."

Her lips curved into the faintest smile. "That's because you weren't looking down."

But I wasn't looking at the river at all. I was looking at her then, really admiring her, and thought that why would I ever need to look anywhere else?

And in that instant, it was clear. We weren't just two strangers who'd stumbled into each other's lives anymore. We had crossed the line, without meaning to or maybe intentionally,

We were in love.

For a long while, we just stood there, listening to the quiet hum of the river below. The world felt vast and silent, yet we had carved out our own small universe on that bridge.

I finally broke the silence, my voice low, almost afraid to disturb the magic of it.

"You know… I'll never forget this place."

She pulled back slightly, her eyes searching mine. "Because of the view?"

I shook my head, smiling faintly. "No. Because of you."

She looked away, a shy laugh escaping her lips, but her fingers squeezed mine just a little tighter.

We walked back slowly toward the bike, still holding hands, neither of us in any hurry to let go. She leaned against the railing for one last glance at the river, her hair brushing against my arm as the wind picked up. Then, almost without realizing, she leaned her head lightly against my shoulder.

For the first time in a long time, I didn't feel like I needed to say something clever, or fill the silence. Just standing there with her was enough.

When we finally got on the bike, she slipped her arms around my waist. Not like before, where it was casual or playful, but tighter, warmer. It felt different now. More real.

The road stretched out ahead, glowing under the streetlights. I could feel her cheek against my back. At one red light, I glanced at the rearview mirror. She was looking at me, a faint smile playing on her lips. She caught me staring, and instead of looking away, she mouthed something. Just one word.

"Idiot."

I chuckled, shaking my head, but inside, my chest felt full—like I was carrying something too big to contain.

The ride stretched longer than it should have, not because of distance, but because I slowed down at every turn, dragged my feet at every stretch of empty road. I wanted this night to last. I wanted the feel of her arms around me to stay etched in memory.

When we finally reached near her home, she didn't get off immediately. She sat for a moment longer, as if deciding something. Without a word, she wrapped her arms around me.

For a second, I froze. Then I let myself sink into it, holding her close, breathing in the faint trace of her perfume mixed with the night air.

When she pulled back just slightly, I couldn't help teasing, "So… not afraid of people's eyeballs anymore?"

She looked up at me, her eyes shining under the streetlight. A small smile tugged at her lips as she whispered,

"I don't care about the world anymore."

Something stirred inside me then, something that had been waiting for the right moment. The words rose to my lips before I could stop them. I love...

But just as they were about to slip out, she pressed a finger gently against my lips and shook her head, her eyes holding mine steady.

"Don't limit this by just three words," she said softly. "It means more than that to me."

"Goodnight," she murmured with the faintest smile, and with that, she turned and walked toward her door.

She turned toward her home, leaving me standing there with my heart pounding. I didn't want her to leave me. I wanted her stay with me for eternity.

From then on, every moment carried a different weight, a sweeter rhythm. The weeks that followed flowed like a dream. Our love grew in a way that was both gentle and unstoppable.

Our calls turned softer, slower. We no longer just talked—we lingered. She'd hum songs on the other side of the line, sometimes drifting in half asleep modes. We didn't miss a chance to kiss each other—sometimes quick, sometimes lingering, sometimes playful. On bike rides when the traffic paused and vehicles were visibly distant, during quiet walks when no one was around, even in the middle of a silly argument that ended with both of us laughing into each other's lips. Even in the most ordinary moments, I'd find myself leaning toward her, and she'd already be waiting.

Every touch felt like a promise. Every glance carried a weight I could feel in my chest. What amazed me most was how natural it became, this closeness, this warmth. Like we weren't just falling in love; we were already living inside it.

And yet, every kiss still felt like the first—unexpected, electric, unforgettable.

Our lunches weren't hurried anymore. She'd sit across the table, teasing me about the way I looked at her, and I wouldn't even deny it. Every time she walked in, it felt like the world tilted a little toward me.

We built tiny traditions. Evening chai at the corner tapri. Friday night pani puri battles. Sunday mornings where I'd show up with her favorite flowers, claiming I "just passed by" even though I'd crossed half the city.

Her new apartment began to feel like my second home. Sometimes I'd fix things. Change a bulb, set up a shelf—but mostly I was there to just be with her. One evening, we sat on her balcony, the city lights flickering below us. She leaned into me, quiet, her fingers tracing lazy patterns on my hand. For a long while, neither of us spoke. And yet, in that silence, I heard everything—her trust, her warmth, her love.

Weeks passed, the feeling only grew. Every day with her felt like a new discovery. Every time we said goodbye after a date, she hugged me tighter. And every time she walked away, I already missed her.

Love wasn't something I was chasing anymore—it was already here, living in the little moments, the glances, the laughter, the comfort of knowing she was mine, and I was hers.

It was the wedding of Karan's brother and the whole group was buzzing with excitement. Weddings were always an excuse for us boys to dress sharp, eat more than we should, drink like crazy and dance like maniacs. But this one felt different. I wasn't just going with the guys this time, Radhika was coming too.

I was waiting for her. Every time someone entered through the decorated gate, my heart jumped—until finally, she walked in.

Radhika came with her friends, draped in a soft saree that made the lights of the wedding hall seem dull in comparison. As she stepped in, someone from the baraat playfully threw flower petals, and for a split second, my mind betrayed me. It wandered far ahead into a future where I could see her walking toward me the same way, only this time as a bride. I couldn't stop staring. The world was blurred, music muted, everything narrowing down to the sight of her.

She looked nervous, though, fidgeting slightly as her eyes scanned the endless crowd of relatives. She saw me and came towards me.

She noticed that I was wandering in my own thoughts. With a blush tugging at her lips, she leaned closer and whispered,

"Stop staring at me like that. I'm your girlfriend, not someone you've just seen for the first time."

I smiled, but deep inside, I knew it wasn't that simple. Every time I saw her, she looked new. Beautiful in a different way, like I was discovering her all over again.

"Don't worry,' I leaned in and said quietly. 'It's not our wedding. You just have to survive the food, music, and nosy aunties, some of them are my relatives too.'

She laughed, shaking her head. "Easy for you to say."

As we sat together watching Karan's brother and his bride on stage, I found myself lost in thought. The mandap fire glowed, the couple exchanged shy glances, and in that moment, I imagined what it would feel like if it were us up there one day.

The evening went on with rituals, laughter, and endless plates of starters. We danced, teased Karan, and celebrated like family. My friends were thrilled to see her there. Teasing me, of course—but she handled it gracefully, even laughing along.

It was then Karan walked up and said, "Hey, your parents are here. Come, I'll take you."

I froze for a second. My parents. I hadn't thought this through.

Radhika immediately picked up on it. "Your parents? They're here?" she asked, her voice a mix of curiosity and nerves.

"Yeah," I nodded slowly. "Do you… want to meet them?'. A few of our friends pushed me, whispering, *"Introduce her to uncle and aunty, yaar. Don't hide her."*

Her eyes widened. She bit her lip, clearly nervous, but she nodded anyway. "If you want me to."

I wanted her to. More than that, I wanted my parents to see her. To know her. To understand why I was smiling differently these days. We walked together toward the corner where my parents were seated, my heart thumping louder with every step. My mother looked up first, her eyes softening as she noticed Radhika walking beside me.

"Maa, pappa" I said, my throat a little dry, "this is Radhika."

For a second, the air felt heavier than it should have. Radhika folded her hands politely and said softly, "Namaste."

My mother's face broke into a warm smile. "So this is Radhika. We've heard about you."

I nearly choked. 'Heard about you'? I hadn't told them anything, but apparently my smiles and late-night phone calls had said enough.

My father gave a small nod, not unfriendly, but reserved. "Sit, beta," he said.

Radhika sat beside me, still a little stiff, but slowly she began to talk when my mother asked her about her work and her family. I watched as she handled every question gracefully, her nervousness melting bit by bit.

At one point, my mother leaned closer and whispered to her, "You look beautiful in that saree."

I saw Radhika's cheeks flush, and my heart swelled.

My dad, more formal, asked her about her job, how she was finding Nashik. I sat beside her, watching her balance her nerves with grace. I saw Radhika not just as the girl I was falling for, but as someone fitting effortlessly into my world.

After a while, my parents excused themselves to greet some friends and relatives. I let out a slow breath I hadn't realized I was holding. "Well… that wasn't as terrifying as I thought."

"Easy for you to say," she scolded softly, her eyes narrowing playfully. "You could've at least told me your parents were going to be here too."

I grinned. "Relax. You handled them better than I ever would have."

We rejoined our friends, and while the stage was getting crowded by guests, we sat quietly in a corner.

"So," she said, leaning closer, "about the thing you said earlier."

"What thing?"

"You told me earlier this isn't our wedding."

I raised an eyebrow. "Yeah, because it's not. Pretty obvious, isn't it?"

She leaned in, eyes twinkling. "Then why were you staring at the couple like you were rehearsing for your own big day?"

I almost choked on my drink. "Excuse me? I was just… observing the rituals. You know, cultural interest. And what makes you think that?"

She tilted her head, eyes sparkling with that knowing look she always had. "Because you had that faraway look in your eyes. I've started to recognize it. You were staring at the couple, but you weren't really seeing them. I bet you were imagining yourself as the groom."

I tried to hide my grin but failed miserably. "Am I that predictable?"

"Yes." she said instantly, laughing softly. Then, after a pause, her tone softened. "Tell me honestly… do you think about our wedding?"

I leaned closer, my tone deliberately teasing. "Hmm… sometimes. But mostly I think about how you'd probably boss me around the entire ceremony."

"Idiot."

I grinned, lowering my voice. "And even if I was imagining, maybe it's because I already know who'd look perfect as the bride."

'You're impossible."

"And you're still stuck with me," I shot back.

She shook her head, still laughing, with her hand lingering on me arm.

CHAPTER 10
NEW BEGINNINGS

LIFE HAS A way of shifting the ground beneath your feet when you least expect it. One moment, you're watching the girl you love laughing with your parents at a wedding, dreaming of futures wrapped in garlands and music. And the next, the same life reminds you that nothing stays untouched forever. Everything you love, everything you hold close, it all changes when time decides to play its game.

We met at our usual café that evening. Radhika sat unusually quiet, her fingers tracing patterns on the table instead of holding her cup. Finally, she slid a folded letter towards me. "I need to tell you something."

I opened it, scanning quickly, and felt my stomach sink. Transfer Order: Mumbai Head Office. Effective next month.

I looked up at her, speechless. She avoided my eyes, biting her lip nervously. "It's not just a promotion. It's… compulsory. They want me in Mumbai. If I decline, they'll probably start looking for someone else."

For a moment, the chatter around us faded. All I could hear was the pounding of my heart. Mumbai. Not another city far away, but still… far enough to take her away from me.'

I tried to keep my voice steady. "So… you don't really have a choice."

She shook her head, her voice breaking. "No. And the worst part is, I don't know what it means for us. I don't want to lose what we have."

Her words cut through me. I wanted to ask her to stay, to fight for us, to find some excuse not to go. But when I looked at her, I saw not just my girlfriend. I saw a young girl building her life, her career, her mother's face came before my eyes, even though I had never seen her. And how could I stand in the way of that?

I reached across the table and took her hand. "You have to go. Not because I want you to, but because you have to. And I don't want you to ever regret choosing me over your future."

Her eyes welled up, "but what about us?"

I squeezed her hand, forcing a smile of my own. "We'll figure it out. Mumbai isn't the end of the world. If our love is real… no distance will break it."

She stirred her coffee without drinking it, her eyes fixed on the swirling foam as if it might carry the answer she wanted to avoid. "I don't want to go," she said firmly, her voice low but steady. "If I accept this transfer, everything between us will change. I know it will."

"Hey… everything will be fine. Trust me. You don't have to be scared of losing us. I'm not going anywhere." I leaned forward, catching her hand again. "Radhika, listen to me. You won't lose me."

She blinked, confused. "What do you mean?"

I took a deep breath, letting the words pour out.

"You know that I am waiting for MBA entrance exam results. They will be out soon. I'll try to get admission in Mumbai. It won't be a problem. Dad has been transferred there since two years now. I can stay with him while studying. That way… you won't have to choose. We can both go to Mumbai. Together."

Her eyes widened, the weight of the world lifting off her in an instant. For a moment, she just stared, as if she hadn't heard me right.

"You'd do that?" she whispered.

I smiled, brushing my thumb across her hand. "I'd do anything not to lose you." Tears welled in her eyes, but for the first time since she got the letter, her lips curved into a real smile.

Later that night, I took her out on my bike. She climbed on behind me, and as we rode through the dimly lit roads. She wrapped her arms around me tighter than ever before. She clung to me so tightly I could feel every beat of her heart against my back. There was something desperate in her hold. Like she was afraid that if she let go, the world would snatch me away.

Convincing my parents wasn't that hard. They were happy with my decision—our son taking the next step in his academics made them proud. So, the packing began. I felt guilty about leaving my mother alone, but she didn't stop me. Instead, she encouraged me to study hard, reminding me it was only for two years.

The day of our departure had arrived. Radhika and I stood at the railway station with her friends. Karan came to drop us off. Her friends had gathered to see her off, their voices laced with laughter and tears all at once. She hugged each one of them tightly, her heart heavy yet full. 'Don't forget us and come back soon and this time with no intention of going away.' one of them teased.

She finally turned toward me she walked slowly, her bag slipping from her shoulder, and in her voice. Her fingers tightened around mine, and in that small gesture, I knew we were carrying each other forward.

Mumbai wasn't Nashik. Not even close.

The city swallowed us whole from the moment we stepped out of the station. Cars honking, Buses rushing by, people moving as if the ground itself was on fire. It smelled of exhaust and something strangely alive. Everything was bigger, louder, faster.

I dropped her off first at her new shared apartment. Her roommates welcomed her with the cautious kindness of strangers who might one day become friends. I watched her carry her bag inside, and when she turned to wave, I caught a glimpse of her trying to mask her nerves with a smile. I smiled back, pretending not to notice.

Then it was my turn. A cab ride across the city took me to my father's rented flat. When I opened the door, silence greeted me. Dad was away for few days attending a meeting. The rooms were empty. For a moment, I just stood there, luggage in hand, listening to my own breath bounce off the walls.

But instead of loneliness, I felt a strange sense of possibility. I had to make a future for me, for us. It was time I took my studies even more seriously and land a decent job as soon as possible. I wanted to give her a better life. No – A great life. And for that I needed to study for the next two years.

That night, the flat felt cavernous and hollow. I dropped onto the sofa. Tried watching television but got bored instantly. I kept staring at the blank ceiling, the hum of Mumbai's traffic leaking in through the window. My phone was the only thing keeping me company, and instinctively, I called her.

"Missing me already?" she teased.

"Obviously," I shot back

"You settled in?"

"Yeah. The girls are nice… the place is okay. But it's not home yet," she said with a small sigh.

"Same here. Dad isn't even in the city. So, it's just me… in this empty flat."

There was silence for half a beat. Then her tone changed slightly, playful. "Wait. Did you just say you're all alone in a flat in Mumbai? And you didn't tell me earlier?"

I laughed softly, already sensing where this was going. "Why? What difference would that have made?"

"Because," she teased, her voice dropping a notch, "if I'd known… maybe I would've come over. At least to keep you company."

My breath hitched, and I sat up, heart thumping. "You're joking."

"Am I?" she said, laughing softly. "You'd never know now, would you? Lost your chance."

I groaned, running a hand through my hair. "Don't say that, Radhika. Now I'm picturing you here. Do you have any idea what that does to me?"

She giggled, "Maybe I do. Maybe that's why I said it. We'll just have to wait till the next chance"

"And when it does," I replied, "I won't let it slip."

Her breath caught faintly, then she whispered, "Goodnight."

'Goodnight.'

The next week in Mumbai was chaos. Radhika and I hadn't met even once. She was swallowed by her new office life, while I was trying to catch up with college routines.

Every morning, I fought the local train schedules. Either missing one by seconds or getting shoved into the next, packed shoulder to shoulder with strangers, the rush hour swallowing any sense of space. By the time I reached college, I was drained, clothes crumpled, mind already half spent

With Dad back in the city, I had taken charge of dinners most nights. Cutting vegetables after long lectures, stirring dal while kneading dough. It became a strange routine I didn't expect to enjoy. Sometimes Dad would come to the kitchen, watching me cook with a faint smile. "Didn't think you had this side in you," he'd remark, and I'd shrug, though secretly proud.

One evening he took me out to dinner at a nearby restaurant. It was the one my dad liked and he knew I would love it too. A simple place with warm lighting and quiet chatter around. The moment I sat there, something tugged at me. The way the plates were set, the hum of people's voices, the way the food arrived steaming hot… it all reminded me of the dinners with her. Of the way she'd smile across the table, hiding her laughter behind her phone, the way she'd tease me over silly things. I found myself staring at the empty seat across from me, imagining her there instead of Dad, and caught myself before he noticed.

Later that night, when she called, I almost told her. Almost told her how every part of this new life sucked and all I could think of was of our days back at home. How the city felt too big and I was lost without her. I just listened to her voice as she complained about how she missed her train again, and I told her how I had burnt the roti at home.

The distance hurt, but in those small calls, those clumsy meals, those crowded rides, I realized that we were both fighting the same city, just on different sides of it. And that kept me going.

Later that night, while lying on my bed, phone pressed to my ear, I asked her, "Do you realize it's been more than two weeks since we last met in person?"

There was a pause on her end, the kind that carried both guilt and longing. "I know," she whispered. "Every evening, I think of calling you to meet, but by the time I'm free, it's either too late or I'm too tired to even move."

I smiled faintly, though my chest ached. "The world is testing us."

She laughed softly. "Then maybe it's time we pass the test. Let's not push it further. This weekend… no matter what, we meet."

"Deal," I said. "No excuses. We owe ourselves that."

"So, where are you taking me on our first outing in Mumbai?

I smiled into the phone, letting my voice drop just a little. "Last time… I missed my chance. Maybe I don't want to miss this one." I didn't need to see her face to know she was smiling, lips pressed together, her heart racing the same way mine was.

Her voice lowered, almost a whisper. "And what makes this time different?"

I hesitated just enough to let the meaning sink in. "Let's just say… there won't be anyone to disturb us and we could do whatever we want."

Finally, she whispered, half-nervous, half-playful, "That sounds dangerous."

'Don't worry," I said, letting my tone drop to a mock seriousness. "I won't bite." Then, after a pause, I added, "Maybe I would."

She laughed again, "You're enjoying this way too much.'

"You can't blame me for that."

After a long pause, she said softly, "So…see you Friday night, then?"

"I can't wait till then." I said.

"Goodnight," she finally whispered, her voice warm, lingering.

"Goodnight," I said softly,

When the call ended, I just laid back on my bed, phone still in my hand, staring at the ceiling. For weeks, I'd replayed the sound of her laugh, the memory of her lips on that bridge, the warmth of her arms around me. And now, for the first time, we'd have the world shut out, just us in the same space, no interruptions, no excuses. I couldn't stop my thoughts from running ahead.

The local train screeched into the station, but all I could hear was my own heartbeat hammering in my chest. It had been weeks. But tonight, she wasn't a voice on the phone. She was real. She was coming back to me. And then I saw her. My breath caught in my throat. She looked beautiful—no, more than beautiful. She looked like every second of waiting had been worth it. And I realized in that instant that maybe she wasn't just more beautiful than I remembered. Maybe love itself was making me see her differently, sharper, brighter, like she carried her own light.

Her eyes found me and her smile broke me apart. I wanted to grab her hand, pull her into me, kiss her right there without caring if half the city was watching,

When she reached me, we didn't speak at first. We just looked at each other, smiling stupidly, like we both knew words would never be enough for this moment.

"Hi," she whispered, soft but shaky, like she felt it too.

"Hi," I breathed back, though what I really wanted to say was God, I missed you. Don't ever leave my side again.

We didn't say much as we walked out together. Words felt too small, too light, to hold what was going on. We were really nervous about the fact that we were going to be alone together for the next weekend. Our hands brushed once, twice, before she slipped hers into mine, and it stayed there, like it belonged.

By the time we reached my flat, my chest was heavy with anticipation. I unlocked the door and stepped aside, letting her in first. I closed the door behind us, suddenly aware that it was just the two of us now, no noise, no city, no interruptions. My voice felt lower, steadier, when I said, "Welcome home."

She looked around, her eyes sweeping over the small living room. It wasn't much. But I had made sure it was clean, organized, almost homely.

"It's… nice," she said softly, turning back to me with a smile. "Small, but cosy. I like how you've kept it." For a moment, she just wandered around the room, running her fingers across the table, pausing at the window to peek out at the view of the city lights.

"This feels… different," she said softly, almost to herself.

I leaned against the wall, watching her. Different?

She turned back and caught me staring. "You've been looking at me like that since the station," she teased, her lips curling into a playful smile.

I grinned but didn't deny it. "Can you blame me? You look…" I paused, searching for the right word, but nothing seemed enough.

For a heartbeat, silence stretched between us, charged, unspoken. Her cheeks flushed, and she brushed her hair behind her ear before walking over and dropping her bag on the sofa.

The closeness made the air shift. My pulse quickened.

"Hungry?" I asked, trying to cut through the tension, though my voice came out rougher than I intended.

She shook her head gently, eyes locked on mine. "Not really."

I nodded, swallowing hard. "Thirsty?"

Her smile deepened, faint but knowing. "No."

Something in her tone told me she wasn't talking about water.

She took a step closer. I couldn't move away. She tilted her head slightly, her eyes softening, and I could feel the distance between us shrinking, second by second. My lips were already parting in anticipation, but just when I thought she would lean in, she stepped back with a playful spark in her eyes.

"Give me a minute… I'll freshen up," she said, leaving me caught between frustration and admiration.

When she returned, it felt like time slowed. She wasn't dressed up anymore, just simple shorts and a thin t-shirt that clung lightly to her perfect figure. Her hair was tied loosely, strands falling over her face, and there was something disarmingly intimate about seeing her like this. Not polished, not formal, just her, and somehow even more beautiful.

I had ordered food by then, trying to distract myself, but the moment she sank onto the sofa beside me, all my practiced calm slipped. She sat close, deliberately close, her bare thigh brushing against me every now and then, sending a current up my spine.

We poured ourselves wine, talked about her new workplace, about the chaos of local trains. But the conversation kept thinning, melting into quiet pauses where our eyes lingered too long. Each laugh ended softer than it began, her gaze dropping to my lips before darting away.

The wine warmed us, but it wasn't the alcohol — it was the air between us. At one point, she shifted closer, curling her leg beneath her, resting her arm on the back of the sofa — her shoulder nearly grazing my cheek. I could smell her shampoo, something faint and floral, and it made my throat tighten.

Finally, there was no stopping it. Her eyes met mine, steady, unblinking, and then she leaned in first. Our lips met, slower than the first time, but deeper, like we both knew there was no reason to hold back anymore.

The kiss grew fiercer, hungrier, until I felt her fingers slide against my jaw, pulling me closer. My hands found her waist, her back, memorizing the warmth of her body pressed to mine. She gasped softly into my mouth, and the sound nearly undid me.

She shifted, half onto my lap now, and I could feel her heartbeat racing as wildly as mine. Every touch was a question, answered instantly by the next touch.

The room grew smaller, quieter, until there was nothing left between us. Clothes slipped away without thought, falling to the floor like barriers we no longer needed. The intensity of it nearly stopped my breath.

When it was over, we lay tangled together, her head on my chest, both of us still catching our breath. The quiet wrapped around us, comfortable and alive with everything unspoken. All I could think about was our journey. From that first awkward "hi" to this moment, where words weren't enough to hold what we felt.

After a while, I tilted my head down. "Can I ask you something?"

She hummed softly, half-asleep against me. "Hmm?"

"What made you stop and talk to me that night?"

She lifted her head, rested her chin on my chest, and a mischievous smile tugged at her lips. "I have something to tell you."

I frowned, curious. "What?"

"Remember my friend Priya?"

"Yes," I said instantly. "She was with you when we went to the lake."

"And do you remember her being at the wedding with me?"

I thought for a moment. "Now that you mention it… yeah. She was standing with you that night."

She nodded. "Right. Actually… she was the one who noticed you at the wedding first. She pointed you out to me."

I blinked. "That's why you looked at me?"

She laughed softly. "Mmhmm. And the funny part? She thought you were really cute. During the whole wedding, we kept whispering that you were checking her out. And when you walked up to me that night, I honestly thought you were going to talk to her."

I groaned, covering my face with one hand. "Oh God. Now I feel guilty. What did she say later?"

"She was a little sad," she admitted, then grinned, "but we laughed about it that same night.'

I let out a breath, shaking my head. "But that doesn't answer my question. What made you… trust me? If I think about it now, I wouldn't blame you for walking away. Some random guy approaching you on a quiet street at night? I mean… it could've gone either way."

Her smile softened, and she rested her cheek against my chest again. "Your voice, Adi."

"My voice?" I asked, surprised.

"Yeah." Her words were almost a whisper. "It had something in it… something that made me want to listen. There was pain in it, and calmness, like you'd been carrying too much but still knew how to hold yourself together. I felt connected to that. And even though you lied to me…" she traced a circle lazily on my chest with her finger, "I could tell that the person behind those words could never hurt me. Girls have that superpower, you know."

For a long moment, I just looked at her, struck by the raw honesty in her voice.

"Wow," I finally whispered. "So, my voice saved me?"

She smiled against me. "And trapped me with you."

We didn't speak after that. Her cheek rested against my chest, her breath warm and steady. For a while, I thought she was simply soaking in the silence with me. But then I realized, she had already slipped into sleep. I smiled to myself, the realization filling me with a strange tenderness. I didn't move an inch, as I didn't want to disturb her. My arm stayed wrapped around her, holding her as if she were the most precious thing I had ever been given.

Carefully, I bent my head and pressed a soft kiss into her hair. The scent of her lingered, calming me in a way nothing else ever had. I closed my eyes, my chest rising and falling in rhythm with hers.

And for the first time in a long time, I felt utterly at peace. No doubts, no worries, just the simple truth that she was here, with me. I was the happiest guy in the world.

The morning, I woke up to the most beautiful scene — her face. Her hair was messy, strands falling across her eyes, but to me, she looked perfect. I whispered softly, "I wish I could wake up to your face every day."

She smiled without opening her eyes and moved even closer, curling against me. We just stayed there, wrapped in the quiet warmth. Eventually, the day pulled us out of bed. We decided to roam the city together, hand in hand, figuring things out like two newcomers chasing small adventures. We squeezed into a crowded local train, laughing every time we lost balance and caught each other. At Marine Drive, we sat by the sea, letting the waves crash against the rocks while the breeze tangled her hair. At Siddhivinayak temple, we joined the lines, prayed quietly, and found a strange comfort in the simplicity of it. Lunch was street food. Hot vada pav and tangy pani puri.

By evening, tired but happy, we carried back food for dinner. That night ended with us in each other's arms, closeness turning into passion.

The next day was Sunday. I asked her if she wanted to go out somewhere, maybe explore more of Mumbai. She shook her head with a little smile. "Let's just spend the day inside… just us."

And so, we did. We cooked together, clumsy but laughing all the way, flour on our hands and spices in my eyes. Every little task became an excuse to lean into each other, to sneak kisses, to laugh like we had no care in the world. The hours blurred, kisses turning into embraces, embraces turning into more. We lost count of how many times we pulled each other close and how many times our clothes went off and on.

It wasn't just a weekend together. It was the beginning of something deeper, something that made both of us feel like we belonged in the city, in life, and in each other's arms.

We got ready slowly, not rushing like we normally would. When it was finally time to leave, we stepped out of the flat together. As we walked to the station, I caught myself thinking: If only every morning started like this. Waking up next to her. Walking to the train together. Living like this forever.

I glanced at her and smiled. "You know, it feels like we're already… living together."

She looked at me, and the corner of her lips curved upward. "Yeah. It feels… nice. Too nice."

"Dangerously nice," I teased. "Like I might get used to it."

She nudged me with her shoulder. "What if you do?"

"Then maybe we should make it permanent someday." I said it casually. She didn't reply immediately, just gave me that shy smile that said she had understood.

At the station, we went our separate ways, waving one last time before the crowd swallowed us. But the thought stayed with me the whole day.

Life in Mumbai slowly shaped itself around us. The chaos of the city no longer felt overwhelming; it became the rhythm of our days. She settled into her new workplace, making friends, carving her own place in the bustling city. I found myself absorbed in classes, assignments, and everything that came with this new chapter.

But no matter how hectic it got, we found our way back to each other. Calls during lunch breaks, evening video calls after long days, and weekends that became our little escapes. Whenever my dad went back to Nashik for a few days, the apartment became ours again.

CHAPTER 11
LEAP OF FAITH

TIME ALWAYS PASSES quickly when you're enjoying it. And now the festival season had arrived. Diwali always made you feel homesick. We were both going home for the holidays—she to Goa, and I to Nashik.

We had a few minutes before her train arrived. The station was buzzing with Diwali rush.

"It's the first time since I met you… that I won't be in the same city as you." I tried to keep my voice light, but it came out softer than I intended.

Her eyes lingered on mine, "You are making me cry."

"I am sorry." I sighed, then looking at her again. "I'm going to miss you."

She gave a small nod, almost a whisper, "Me too."

The announcement echoed overhead, and soon her train rolled in with a screech. I carried her luggage inside, weaving through the crowd until we found her seat. She stood at the doorway, holding the iron bar, and reached out for my hand. I didn't let go.

"I'll be leaving for Nashik tomorrow," I told her.

"Okay," she said softly, her thumb brushing against mine.

"Call me once you reach," I reminded, even though I knew she would.

She looked straight at me, her voice steady but her eyes glistening just a little. "I love you, Adi."

My chest tightened. I squeezed her hand, smiling even as the lump in my throat threatened to choke me. "Love you too."

The whistle blew, and slowly the train began to move. I walked along for a few steps, still holding her hand until the space widened, and I had to let go. She leaned out the window, waving, and I waved back until she disappeared into the blur of the platform crowd.

The next morning, I packed my bag and left for Nashik. The city greeted me with the familiar chaos of Diwali. Houses lit up with lanterns, rangolis brightening every doorstep, the smell of sweets everywhere. For the next few days, I let myself get lost in the warmth of family, the laughter of cousins, the sparkle of firecrackers.

She too was home, wrapped in the same kind of festive whirlwind. Yet no matter how crowded our houses were, our nights belonged only to us. We slipped away into phone calls after dinner, whispering under blankets, sharing the details of our days, filling the gap the distance had created.

"You know," she said suddenly, "Goa is beautiful this time of year. The fields are green after the rains, and the beaches aren't too crowded yet. Everyone says it feels like the best season to visit."

I laughed softly. "Are you selling Goa as if I've never heard of it?"

"No," she replied, her tone playful but careful. "I'm just saying… maybe you should see it. My village, my side of Goa. It's very different from what you've seen in pictures. It's… home."

There was a pause. My heart thumped at the word. Home.

"Are you inviting me?" I asked.

"Not exactly," she teased. "But if you did decide to come, maybe you'd finally meet my mother. She keeps asking about you, you know."

The thought rooted itself in me immediately. Meeting her mother. It wasn't just about us anymore; it was about the world around us beginning to merge. A step forward.

I smiled into the silence. "Then maybe I don't have a choice, do I? If Goa looks this beautiful, and your mother is already curious, I think I should see both."

Her laugh was soft and shy, almost as if she had been waiting for me to say it.

"Let's see if you're brave enough, Adi."

Goa was on.

But the truth was, when I first thought of it, I imagined Goa the way most boys do — loud, carefree, beaches and bikes, a trip with the gang. Still, this time there was a different reason tucked quietly in my chest.

I laid the plan before the boys one evening.

Karan raised an eyebrow. "Oh, so now you want to go to Goa? Two years ago when I suggested it, you shot me down. What changed, huh? Or should I say… who changed?" He smirked knowingly.

I tried to brush it off. "Shut up, Karan. It'll be fun, that's all."

"Fun? Or Radhika fun?" he pressed, making Bharat and Nishant burst into laughter.

Bharat, as always, was the cautious one. "I don't know, yaar. These trips take planning. Expenses, time…"

Before he could finish, Karan threw an arm around him dramatically. "Arre, Bharat baba, don't kill the vibe! Think of the beaches, the seafood, the late-night guitar on the sand! You'll thank me later."

Even Nishant, who had been quietly sipping his chai, chimed in. "Bharat, stop overthinking. It's Goa, every boy's group need a Goa trip."

By the end of the evening, the plan was sealed.

When I told my parents it was a boys' trip, they didn't object. Maybe they trusted that Karan's loud presence would balance out my quieter one. Or maybe they just thought that finally, Adi is living a little.

Next thing we knew, we were boarding the train to Goa, bags slung on our shoulders, energy buzzing through the air. Karan was already cracking jokes, Nishant had his earphones in, and Bharat was double-checking tickets like a worried parent.

But me? Beneath all the noise and laughter, my heart was drumming for one reason only — Radhika.

The train finally screeched into Madgaon station, the air instantly heavy with salt and heat. We grabbed our bags, laughed our way out. We were rolling down the palm-fringed roads of Goa in a rattling cab, Karan and Nishant already arguing about who'd be the last man standing tonight.

By evening, we reached Calangute. The beach stretched wide and golden, waves catching the last glow of the sun. Our cottage sat just a few steps away from the shore — small, wooden, with a porch that looked like it belonged in a movie.

"Boys, Goa is officially conquered!" Nishant yelled, arms wide open.

Karan threw his bag on the sand. "First order of business—beers!"

Their laughter filled the air as they raced inside to claim their beds. I stayed back, phone buzzing in my hand. Her name lit up the screen.

I answered, voice softening instantly. "Hey. We've reached."

"Finally," Radhika's voice came, warm, teasing. "How's Goa treating you so far?"

"Not bad," I said, glancing at Karan already pulling out the cans of beer. "The boys are acting like kids set loose in a candy shop."

She laughed, then her tone shifted just slightly, enough to make me straighten. "Listen… don't drink too much tonight. Tomorrow you are coming home for the first time. And I don't want you showing up with red eyes and a hangover."

"I'll behave," I said softly. "Promise."

"Good," she replied, her voice lighter again.

And then, the night then blurred into laughter, music, and the cool air. Karan and Nishant had dragged me into their madness. Unlimited beer, loud dancing on the sand, and ridiculous dares. We stumbled back to our cottage sometime past two, the world spinning just enough to feel like freedom.

Morning came too early. My head was still heavy when her name lit up my phone, dragging me out of half-sleep.

"Wake up, sleepyhead," she said. "I'll pick you up in an hour."

And just like that, all traces of hangover vanished.

An hour later, I spotted her weaving through the morning crowd on her moped. Helmet strapped, hair tied back, a bright kurti over jeans. She looked effortless, like Goa itself had dressed her. She stopped, pulled her helmet off, and before I could say a word, she ran into my arms.

"God, I missed you," she whispered, holding me tighter than usual.

I grinned, brushing her hair away from her cheek. "Wait, wait—since when can you ride a scooter? What else are you hiding from me?"

Her eyes sparkled mischievously. "There are many things you don't know yet."

I laughed. "Alright then, hop back. Let me drive. Can't have my girlfriend chauffeuring me around."

She smirked, shaking her head as she handed me the spare helmet. "Nope. Not happening. This is my territory. You sit back and behave."

"Can't promise that." I replied.

And with that, I climbed on behind her, wrapping my arms around her waist.

"Adi," she said suddenly, her voice half-playful, half-warning over her shoulder, "remove your hands."

I blinked. "What? Why?"

"Because you'll distract me. Sit properly."

Reluctantly, I loosened my grip, resting my hands on either side instead, pretending to sulk. "Fine. But just so you know, this is the most unsafe driving arrangement ever."

She laughed, the sound carried by the breeze. "Relax. You're in my Goa now. Nothing happens without my say."

The road narrowed as we turned into her village. The noise of the city disappeared almost instantly. Houses stood tucked between groves of coconut and jackfruit trees, their bright red tiled roofs gleaming in the sun. Whitewashed walls lined with small verandas with wooden chairs, and narrow lanes where kids played chasing each other while dogs barked lazily at the side.

Her home stood at the end of a winding lane, painted in grey with green window frames, a sloping terracotta roof, and a little front porch shaded by vines. A tulsi plant sat proudly in the courtyard, its base painted in white and red. The gate creaked as she pushed it open, and my breath stopped with nervousness. The courtyard smelled faintly of wet earth and incense. A woman emerged, wiping her hands on the edge of her saree.

She looked to be in her fifties, the kind of woman whose life was written not in words but in the lines etched across her face. Her skin was browned from years under the Goan sun, her frame lean from endless days of household work that never seemed to end. Yet, there was something unbreakable about her presence — like no matter how much life demanded, she still had more to give. Her eyes caught me first — sharp, observant, but tired in a way that only years of carrying a family's weight could make them. They sparkled faintly with warmth, and in that instant, I could see exactly where Radhika had inherited her grace.

"Arey beta, you've come!" she said with a smile that was both gentle and welcoming, as if she had known me for years instead of meeting me for the first time. "Come in, come in. Don't stand outside like a stranger."

I smiled back, instantly at ease. "Namaste, Aunty."

"Namaste," she returned, her voice kind. She guided me toward a wooden chair in the small drawing room. The cushions were old but neatly arranged, the whole room radiating the quiet pride of someone who cared deeply for her home.

"You must be tired from the ride," she said, glancing at me with a mother's concern. Then she turned to Radhika with the authority only mothers could carry. "Go, get him a glass of water. He must be thirsty."

Radhika rolled her eyes playfully but obeyed, disappearing into the kitchen.

Her mother turned her gaze back to me, but it wasn't a questioning look. It was soft, reassuring, like she was silently telling me I was welcome here.

"I have heard a lot about you from Radhika… how supportive you were when she was in Nashik, and how you made her life a little easier." She paused, the corners of her lips lifting in a faint smile. "Thank you for that Beta."

I smiled awkwardly, "aunty, honestly… she's a brave girl. She managed herself just fine without help. I did the least I could."

"She's always been strong-willed," her mother began, voice soft, almost nostalgic. "From a very young age, even after your father passed. I knew that I couldn't always be around her. I wanted her to grow up making her own choices, understanding the world, learning to stand on her own."

I nodded, listening intently. "Radhika is… incredible. She's confident, thoughtful… I can see where she gets it from."

Her mother smiled faintly, a mix of pride and lingering sadness in her eyes. "I didn't want her to leave home and live in an unknown city. Part of me always feared the world could be harsh… but I also knew I couldn't hold her back. She had to find her own path. I made sure she knew how to make good decisions for herself, and she did. She listens, but she also trusts her instincts. And I think… she's turned out better than I could have imagined."

I felt a warmth in my chest, a quiet admiration for the woman who had raised the girl I loved. "You did an amazing job, Aunty. I can see it in how she moves through life… with courage, honesty… and kindness."

Radhika returned then, balancing a small tray with a glass of water and a plate of biscuits. She smiled at the two of us and placed the tray on the table.

"Thank you," I said, taking the glass.

We talked for a while about my family. Her mother insisted on staying for lunch. I couldn't decline her. Food was simple but full of flavor, the kind that makes you forget every fancy restaurant meal. The aroma of freshly cooked fish filled the small dining space.

"Aunty," I said, smiling wide, "this is honestly the best fish I've ever had in my life."

Her mother chuckled, clearly pleased. "It's just home cooking. Nothing special." That is what makes it special, I thought. Mothers all around the world are same. They just want to see us happy.

The afternoon went by in soft conversations, laughter, and small stories about village life. It was almost evening and I needed to get back to the boys. Radhika was already grabbing her scooter keys when her mother turned to me. "How did you like our home?"

"It feels like home, Aunty," I said sincerely. "Warm, peaceful… just the kind of place where you never want to leave."

Her mother's expression softened at that. I added, "You must visit Nashik sometime. My family would love to host you there."

She nodded with a smile. "Maybe I will. It's been years since I've stepped out anywhere."

We said our goodbyes and started our ride back. By the time we reached the cottage, the sun was dipping lower.

"So, what's your grand plan now?" she asked.

I grinned, stretching my arms. "Simple. Drink with the boys, roam the beach till we can't walk anymore, and crash at the cottage like kings."

She rolled her eyes, shaking her head. "Uff. That's what every group of boys does when they come to Goa. Cheap beer, loud music, and walking half-dead by sunset."

"Hey," I defended myself, laughing. "That's tradition. It's sacred to us."

'Well,' she leaned closer, "how about I show you a different version of Goa?' My Goa?"

I raised my brows, instantly curious. "Your Goa?"

"Yes," she said firmly, with a spark in her eyes. "And I have a little surprise set for you in the afternoon. Something special. Let your friends tag along too, we'll all have fun. I'll drop you back by evening."

I couldn't help but smile at her confidence. "Hmm, sounds like you're planning to steal me away from my boys."

"Maybe," she teased, brushing her hair back. "Or maybe I just want you to see that Goa isn't just about bars and beaches. There's more to it."

I looked at her for a second longer, knowing she was serious beneath the playfulness. Then I nodded. "Alright, done. I'll convince the boys."

She laughed, the sound mixing with the crashing waves. "Trust me, Adi. They'll thank me by the end of the day."

The next morning, we were on the move. We had rented bikes. Nishant and Karan sharing one, Bharat riding solo, and me hopping onto the back of Radhika's scooter. She was grinning ear to ear, her scarf fluttering in the wind as she took the lead.

Goa unfolded before us, not the touristy postcard version but the raw, quieter side. Narrow village lanes flanked by swaying coconut trees, stretches of silent beaches where the sand was soft and untouched, waterfalls hidden behind winding trails. At one spot, we dipped our feet into cold rushing water, Karan almost slipping and making everyone burst into laughter.

We devoured local food from roadside shacks. Fish thali served on steel plates, kokum sharbat that cooled us instantly. The boys clicked dozens of candid pictures: Bharat dozing off against a rock, Nishant posing dramatically by the sea, Radhika laughing mid-bite, and the two of us caught holding hands when we thought no one was looking.

By afternoon, with the sun mellowing down, curiosity got the better of me. While Radhika was parking the scooter under the shade of a banyan tree, I leaned closer.

"So…" I asked, narrowing my eyes. "What about that big secret you were talking about yesterday? Don't think I've forgotten."

Her lips curved into a mischievous smile. "Patience, Mr. Adi. You'll see."

We rode again, this time deeper inland, the air turning cooler, the road lined with dense greenery. After nearly half an hour, we stopped by a vast lake. The boys were already wide-eyed, looking ahead.

In the middle of the lake stood a tall iron structure, towering high, with thick cables stretching across. A platform hung over the water, and a group of people were gathered, some screaming, some cheering.

Karan let out a whistle. "No way… this is—"

"Bungee jumping," Radhika finished, grinning proudly.

My jaw dropped as I looked at her. "You brought us here? Are you serious?"

She laughed. "I told you I'd show you my version of Goa. This is a part of it. Adventure, not just beer bottles and sand."

"I thought the secret was of we doing something together. Alone.' I whispered in her ear."

"We are going to do this together." She replied.

I stared at the towering structure, my stomach doing flips just looking at it. "You're insane," I muttered, still not taking my eyes off the platform. Radhika, standing right beside me, folded her arms with that same mischievous grin.

"I thought you loved me," I said dramatically, half-teasing, half-hoping she'd let me off the hook.

She tilted her head, her eyes soft but unyielding. "Of course I do. That's exactly why I'm going to do it with you."

Karan put a hand dramatically on my shoulder. "Adi, it was good knowing you. A good man. Brave heart. May your soul rest in peace."

I shot him a glare, but my voice betrayed me. "Guys, I'm not… I don't really do heights."

Before the teasing could continue, I felt her fingers slip into mine. Radhika's touch was firm, grounding. She looked at me, her eyes steady and warm.

"Adi," she whispered, close enough that the noise around us blurred. "Trust me. I'll hold onto you. Nothing will happen. I would never let anything happen to you."

Her words didn't erase the fear, but they quieted it, gave it shape. I wasn't doing this because I wanted to conquer heights. I was doing it because she was here, because she believed in me more than I did myself.

When the harness was strapped on and we began the slow walk up the ramp, my throat went dry. Every step made the ground seem further away, my mind screaming at me to turn back. But then I felt her squeeze my hand. Small, steady squeezes, like secret code: I'm here. I'm with you.

We reached the edge. The wind tugged at my shirt, my heart hammered so hard it felt like it would break free. I couldn't look down. My legs trembled.

"Close your eyes if you have to," she murmured, smiling. "We'll jump together."

The countdown began behind us. Three… two… one…

I shut my eyes tight as we leapt, the world dropping away beneath me. For a split second, panic flooded every vein in my body. I thought my chest would explode. My stomach twisted, like it had leapt out of me and stayed behind on the platform. A raw, primal scream clawed at my throat, but it never came out.

But then her scream of laughter beside me, her hair whipping in the wind, her hand crushing mine. I forced my eyes open, and all I could see was her. Just her. Her hair lashed across her face, her eyes squeezed shut for a second, then opening, wide and shining. She looked at me mid-fall, and in that glance I forgot we were plummeting. Her smile, wild and fearless. Her eyes shining with freedom. It was just her and me, suspended in a rush of air and light.

The fear didn't vanish all at once. It transformed. Every wave of terror turned into a surge of adrenaline, into something brighter, sharper. The wind didn't feel like an enemy anymore. It felt like freedom, like it was lifting us higher instead of dragging us down.

And for the first time, I wasn't thinking about the ground waiting for us. I was thinking how this moment, this freefall with her by my side, felt like the purest thing I had ever known. I realized I wasn't falling anymore. I was flying with her.

The cord stretched, snapped us back, and we bounced like ragdolls in the air. My lungs finally remembered to breathe, pulling in sharp, ragged gasps as the rush thundered through me. My heart felt like it was still falling, even though the ground was pulling us back.

Radhika's laughter echoed over the lake, wild, carefree, infectious. As we dangled there, swaying slowly over the water, I turned to look at her. Her cheeks flushed, eyes bright, strands of hair flying everywhere.

Dangling there above the water, I turned to her, my throat tight. My voice cracked when I whispered, 'I…I.

She smiled, her eyes sparkling even through the rush. 'I love you too,'

When we finally touched the ground, my legs buckled, but before I could stumble, I pulled her into my arms and held on like I never wanted to let go. She was laughing, breathless, but I couldn't laugh. Not yet. My heart was too full.

The boys stared at me like I had just grown wings.

"Damn, Adi actually jumped," Karan muttered, half in disbelief, half impressed.

"Good guy. Brave guy. Mad guy," Nishant added.

Bharat just shook his head, smiling, "Never thought I'd see this day."

I didn't say much. My chest was still heavy from the experience.

The ride back to the cottage was unusually quiet. The boys were tired, cracking the occasional joke, but I barely registered them. Radhika sat behind me on her scooter this time, her hand lightly resting on my shoulder, and even that single touch felt like a reassurance, like she knew exactly where my mind was.

Back at the cottage, the boys collapsed into the chairs and beds, groaning about the long day, already arguing over whether to nap or go hunting for beers.

The sun was still up with some time left for sunset. The beach was quieter now, the waves gentler, like even the sea was catching its breath. We walked side by side, barefoot in the sand, our shoulders brushing now and then.

Neither of us spoke at first. The silence wasn't empty though. I finally glanced at her, and she was already looking at me, a small smile tugging at her lips, as if she knew exactly what was going on in my head.

"Thank you for today. In fact, thank you for everything."

I kept my eyes fixed on the sea, the waves crashing endlessly against the shore.

"The last time I stood before the ocean, I had lost so much… and now, I feel like I've found everything in you. I'm lucky to have you, Radhika. You've made me the happiest person alive. But something about this view—" I paused, my voice trembling, "—it shakes me. It reminds me how fragile all this is. I've lost before, and I fear one day, time might take it all away again. And if that happens, I'm not sure I'd know how to survive it."

"Shhh… don't say another word."

Her finger touched my lips, silencing me with warmth.

"I know life has tested you. It has tested me too. But look where it brought us, right where we were meant to be. Some things had to end so better things could take their place. I could've stayed in Goa, never stepped into your city… but I did. And that decision led me to you."

Her voice softened, eyes shimmering.

"There was a time I thought I'd never love again. Yet here I am, with the most caring man I've ever known. So let me tell you this — I love you from the bottom of my heart, Aditya. Nothing will ever come between us. You're stuck with me till the very end of our time."

I couldn't speak. The sun was dipping into the horizon, painting the sky in gold and crimson. I leaned in, and our lips met. There's something timeless about kissing the love of your life on a beach. The wind brushing your face, the waves roaring around you, and the sunset making her glow like an angel.

We held hands as we walked back from the shore, our footprints side by side in the wet sand.

"So, what's the big plan for tomorrow?" I asked, stealing a glance at her.

She wrapped her hand over my shoulder, leaning in. "Tomorrow is your last day here. So I will let you boys enjoy your trip."

"What? No. The boys enjoy your company."

She shook her head, a playful smile on her lips. "I have already taken a lot of your time and I don't want your friends to dislike me. So enjoy the day. Have fun getting drunk and don't do anything stupid. I will meet you the next morning before your train back."

"That's not fair. How about we stay the night somewhere else?" I said, trying my luck.

She rolled her eyes. "Stop acting cute. It's getting late, Mom might be waiting for me."

By the time we reached the cottage gate, the lights inside told me the boys were already waiting. She lingered for a moment, her hands still resting on my shoulder. Then she stepped back, started her scooter, and with one last smile said, "Goodnight, Adi."

I stood there, watching until her tail light disappeared down the road, before I finally turned and walked in.

The next day passed in a blur of beaches and forts. We roamed, laughed and let the Goan sun soak into our skin one last time. By the time we returned to the cottage that night, the air was alive with music and the smell of the sea. Karan was already half-dancing with Nishant, both of them swaying with bottles in hand, while the speaker blared old Bollywood songs.

I couldn't join in. Not really. My body was there, but my heart was somewhere else. I found myself standing at the gate of our cottage, leaning against the wooden frame, staring out at the sea under the moonlight.

Behind me, laughter echoed, beer bottles clinked, and feet shuffled to music. But I felt oddly detached, as if the night was moving past me while I stood still.

"Why are you looking like some tragic hero from a 90s movie?" Karan's voice came from behind. When I turned, he was holding two bottles of beer, one in each hand. Without waiting for me to answer, he handed me one.

I took it, opening it with a small smile. "Just… watching."

He leaned against the gate beside me, taking a long sip. For a while, we both stared at the sea in silence, letting the distant music fade into the background.

"You're thinking about her, aren't you?" he finally asked.

I hesitated, then gave a small nod.

"So… are you going to propose?"

I froze, the bottle halfway to my lips. "What?"

"You heard me." He nudged my arm.

I couldn't lie to him. "The thought came to my mind yesterday when we were on the beach," I admitted, my voice low. "it's just not that simple. Life doesn't let me hold onto the things I want the most. And I don't have my feet grounded yet. The years I've wasted… they're haunting me now."

I took a shaky breath, my eyes fixed on the moonlit horizon. "It's just… when I look at her, I feel like she's too good to be true. She's two steps ahead of me in life and I don't want to hold her back. I don't want the distance between us to grow either. Don't get me wrong, I do want to marry her. But I'm scared, Karan. I'm really scared."

Karan, for once, didn't jump in with a joke. He just nodded slowly, taking a deep sip of his beer. Then, almost in a whisper, he said,

"You know what I think? You're scared because you finally found something worth losing. And that's how you know it's real." I closed my eyes for a moment, his words cutting through me.

"She already chose you, didn't she? Who are you to argue with her choice?"

"Hmm. When did you get so wise?"

He smirked. "Don't tell anyone. I've got a reputation to keep. Now come back inside."

The night didn't end for a while. We lost the count of beers we had. I am pretty sure it might be some kind of a record. The music was sad but our dance was not. Alcohol has that effect on you. It can make any song turn into a dance number.

The next morning was heavy with drowsy eyes and aching heads. We stuffed our bags into the back of a cab and rode silently to Madgaon railway station, the roads blurring past as the boys trying to doze off in the backseat.

We found a quieter corner near the waiting area of the station.

"You don't look like you slept at all," she teased, her tone half-concerned.

"We were playing a game—who has the worst hangover in the morning."

"Who won?" she raised an eyebrow.

"I think we all lost."

She laughed, then her eyes softened. "Will you miss me?"

"Nope. But I'll most certainly miss Goa."

She swung her hand to punch me, but I caught it midair and held it.

"When are you coming back to Mumbai?" I asked, trying to sound casual.

"In a few days. Maybe just before the weekend."

A smile tugged at my lips. "That's all the answer I need."

At that moment, the train's horn echoed through the station. The boys started gathering their bags, calling out to me. I didn't move. My hand still held hers.

Her grip tightened for the briefest moment, as though asking me not to let go just yet. She hugged me tightly before I boarded, her arms lingering just long enough to make me wish the train would delay forever. Then, with one last look, we were off.

It's strange how time works. One moment, life feels perfect. Like the universe has finally given you everything you ever asked for. But time has a way of testing and taking away what you hold the dearest. It had already defeated me multiple times. It creeps silently, and before you even notice, the ground beneath your feet begins to shift. Sometimes, you don't see the cracks until they've already swallowed you whole.

I wondered, almost guiltily, if I had been too happy. As if life, in its balance, would one day demand a price for all that I had been given. And yet, with her, I dared to hope that maybe, just maybe, I could escape that toll this time.

CHAPTER 12

FATE INTERVENED

VACATIONS ENDED, BUT the memories of Goa remained etched in me. Back to routine, back to cities that never paused. I reached Mumbai two days before her. With Dad in Nashik, the apartment was ours alone.

On Saturday night, we laid together on the bed, her head resting on my chest, our breaths finding a quiet rhythm in the silence of the room. After a long silence she spoke in a fragile whisper.

"You know… before my dad passed, he was bedridden for many days. I used to lay my ear on his chest, just to check if his heart was still beating… just to make sure he was still there."

And then I felt it her tears, warm and silent, rolling down onto my chest. I didn't know how to react or to say. I just held her tighter, my hand pressing gently against the back of her head, as though I could shield her from memories that refused to let go.

Her pain carved itself into me. I wanted to promise her forever, to swear that I'd never leave her, never let her feel that emptiness again. I couldn't take away the sad memories but I wanted to give her lifetime of happy memories.

She sniffled softly against my chest, her breath shaky but trying to steady itself. After a pause, she whispered,

"Mom was asking about you."

My hand froze for a second in her hair. "About me?"

She nodded, not lifting her head. "She… she asked if there was anything between us. If you were just a friend or… something more."

I stayed quiet, waiting, afraid of what she might say next.

"She didn't want me to come back to Mumbai," her voice thick with unspoken conflict. "She wants me to stay close and look for a job nearby. She says she's getting older and she just wants to see me settled… married… while she's still here."

Her words landed heavy in the room, like the silence that follows a storm. I lifted her chin gently, forcing her eyes to meet mine. They were red, glistening, uncertain.

"And what do you want, Radhika?"

Her lips trembled before the words came. "I don't know… I really don't know. I want to be with you. I want this" she pressed her palm against my chest, right where my heart was still beating fast, "but I can't ignore her either. She's all I have left."

For a fleeting second, I wished the world was simpler, that love alone could silence expectations, silence fear, silence the ticking clock of life. But all I could do was hold her closer, my words barely more than a whisper. Her eyes filled again, and she buried herself against me, as if trying to shield both of us from a future neither of us dared to name. The silence between us was heavy, only broken by the sound of her breath against my chest. My arms tightened around her almost instinctively. And before I could stop myself, the words tumbled out,

"I think we should get married."

She froze for a moment, then lifted her head, her tear-streaked face softening into the faintest smile. A small laugh escaped her, though it was laced with disbelief.

"That's a great way to propose," she teased, brushing her hair back from her face.

But then her expression grew serious, almost tender, as she placed her palm against my cheek.

"Don't be silly," she said softly. Then her tone settled, steady and warm. "Listen to me."

"I want us," she began, searching my eyes. "But not like this. Not as a panic button. I don't want our marriage to be an answer to fear. I want it to be a choice. Our choice."

She rested her forehead to mine. "You're still building yourself, Adi. Stand on your own feet and be proud of the ground under you. I want the first time you ask me to be in daylight, when your voice doesn't shake, when you're smiling because you know you're ready."

Her fingers slipped down to my chest, feeling my heartbeat. "And there's my mother. I can't just hand her a decision and say, 'Accept it.' I want her blessing, Adi. Maybe not today, maybe not easily, but I want to try the right way."

She took a breath, eyes shining but certain. "Let's tell them—both sides—when we're steady. Let's give ourselves a foundation first. Save a little. Plan a little. Prove to ourselves that we can hold each other without leaning so hard we both fall."

Her smile wobbled, tender and teasing all at once. "And when you do ask… I want to remember everything about it. Not a dark room and swollen eyes. I want the sun, or rain, or a stupid baloon—whatever you decide—but I want to say yes to joy, not to fear."

Her words sank into me slowly, like drops of water seeping through stone. Every sentence was both a balm and a wound. She was right, she always was. And yet, all I could feel was the ache of how much I wanted to hold on to her forever, right here, right now.

I let out a shaky laugh that wasn't really a laugh. "You make it sound so simple," I whispered, though my throat was tight. "Like all I need is time, and everything will fall into place."

Inside, though, my chest was on fire. Because time, time had never been kind to me. Time had a way of snatching away what I loved most. My father's broken expectations, my wasted years chasing nothing, the shame of being the boyfriend who still hadn't 'made it.' And now, the fear that life might notice how happy I was with her and decide to punish me for it.

I turned my face into her hair, breathing her in, as though her scent alone could anchor me. "You don't understand, Radhika," I murmured. "When I look at you, I feel like… like I'm standing on the edge of something too beautiful for me. And part of me keeps waiting for the ground to give way."

She held on tighter, but I could still feel the tremor in my voice as I went on. "You say not now, and you're right. I know you're right. But it scares me. Because I've spent years running in circles, and what if by the time I finally stand on my own feet… you're not here anymore? What if I lose you before I even get the chance to deserve you?"

My eyes stung, and I shut them hard, pressing my lips to her forehead. "I'm not strong like you. I pretend I am, but inside… I'm terrified. Terrified of failing, of falling short, of being the reason you end up with regrets instead of happiness."

I pulled her closer, almost desperately, as if she might slip away if I loosened my grip even a little. And then, softer than a prayer, I whispered, "I don't know if I'll ever be enough for you, Radhika. But I swear, I'll spend whatever time I get trying."

"Adi," Her eyes glistened in the dim light, but her voice held no hesitation. "I'm here because of you. Because even with all your fears, even with your chaos, you've given me more love and care than I ever thought I'd deserve. And don't talk about deserving—love isn't an exam you pass. It's not a medal you win. It's just… two people deciding, again and again, to choose each other. That's all."

I swallowed hard, her words cutting through my storm. She pressed her palm against my chest, over my heart, as if to steady it. "You think you're not strong, but do you know how much strength it takes to love someone while carrying all that fear? To me, you've only ever been the safest place I've known."

Her voice cracked then, tears brimming, but she didn't look away. "Don't ever think you're not enough for me, Aditya. You are my peace, my madness, my today, and my tomorrow. And even if tomorrow scares you, I want to walk into it with you. Only you."

She leaned in, her lips trembling against mine, and when she kissed me, it wasn't just affection, it was a vow.

Life settled into its old rhythm. Familiar, yet strangely heavier. I drowned myself in my books, while she slipped into her long office hours. Our worlds ran on parallel tracks, meeting only in the small pockets of time we carved out for each other.

Sometimes, it was a hurried lunch near her office, her hair tied up in a messy bun, eyes tired from staring at screens. Other times, it was late at night, when she would call me half-asleep, her voice softer than the silence around me.

"Adi, are you studying or staring at the walls again?" she'd ask, teasing.

"Both," I'd reply, just to hear her laugh.

The exams were drawing closer, and my life had become a cycle of scribbled notes, cold tea, and restless nights. My desk was buried under textbooks, sticky notes, and highlighters that had lost their brightness weeks ago. Every morning began with the same ritual—flipping through chapters I thought I had mastered, only to realize I hadn't retained a thing.

One afternoon, she dragged me out of that suffocating cycle and into a small café near her office. The place smelled of strong coffee and butter-laced sandwiches. For a few moments, my stress melted away. Just her laughter and the warmth of coffee between us.

That weekend, she came over while I was still buried in my notes. At some point, she dozed off beside me, her head resting on my shoulder, strands of hair brushing against my cheek. I wanted to stop time, keep her right there, safe, close, mine.

But time never listens.

After a few days, we went back to the same café. She stirred her cold coffee absentmindedly, tracing circles in the froth with her spoon. I was rambling about my upcoming paper, already mapping out the chapters I'd revise again that evening, when she suddenly said, almost offhand—

"You won't believe who I ran into back in Goa."

I looked up, the words halting in my throat. "Who?"

She hesitated, then shrugged, pretending it wasn't important. "Rohan."

Her ex. The name hung in the air like smoke. I tried to mask the stiffness in my jaw, nodding as if it were nothing. "Oh."

"Yeah, just a quick hello. He asked how I've been. That's it." She smiled faintly, trying to make it sound like small talk. "We didn't even talk much."

But her fingers betrayed her, fidgeting with the spoon, tapping it against the glass.

I nodded again, forcing a smile. "Right. Just a hello."

She reached for my hand across the table. "Don't overthink it."

Her touch was warm, reassuring, but something in me stayed cold. I wanted to believe her. I did. And yet, somewhere deep inside, that name had already carved out a space, a shadow I couldn't ignore.

A week later, she dragged me into a crowded street. The market was a chaos of colors and voices. Stalls spilling over with kurtis, dupattas, sandals, and shopkeepers shouting out discounts as if the world depended on it.

Radhika, of course, was in her element. She darted from one stall to another, bargaining like she had been born with the skill. Every time I thought she was done, she'd spot another piece of fabric or a pair of earrings that *"would go perfectly with this top."*

Meanwhile, I was reduced to her unofficial porter. My both arms weighed down with bulging bags, some digging into my wrists.

"Are you done yet?" I groaned, shifting the bags to keep circulation in my fingers.

She turned, a playful grin on her face. "You're complaining now, but wait till you see me wear all of this. You'll forget the weight."

"By then I'll probably need surgery on my shoulders," I muttered, but she caught the smile I couldn't hide.

At one point, a shopkeeper handed her a mirror to try a scarf. She turned toward me, the scarf draped across her shoulders, her face glowing in the golden bulbs strung across the stall. For a moment, the noise of the market dimmed, and all I saw was her—beautiful, carefree, alive.

"Don't just stare, help me decide!" she snapped me out of it, laughing.

I shifted the bags to one arm and pretended to inspect her.

"Nope. Nothing suits you. You look terrible."

By the time we were done with the bazaar, I looked like a walking mannequin stand. My fingers had gone red from the weight of all the bags, and Radhika still darted from stall to stall with the same energy she had two hours ago.

"Radhika," I groaned, "this isn't shopping, this is a full-body workout."

She turned, arms crossed, fighting back a laugh. "Oh, come on, Mr. Cricketer. You can run for hours behind a ball but can't carry a few bags for me?"

"A few?" I raised my hand to show her the marks left on my palm. "I've got battle scars."

She slipped her arm through mine, pulling me away from the crowd. "Okay, enough. Let's go somewhere quiet before you faint dramatically in the middle of the market."

We walked until the noise faded and the sea breeze began to cut through the sticky air. The streetlights behind, dotting the curve of the Queen's Necklace. For a moment, they reminded me of fireflies—tiny, fragile lights fighting against the night. I dropped the bags beside the stone ledge with a relieved sigh, rubbing my sore hands.

"You see?" she teased, sitting down beside me. "All worth it for this view."

I leaned against the ledge, catching my breath. "You know, the sea here is different from Goa's."

Her eyebrows arched. "Different? How?"

"In Goa, the sea feels… free. Wild. Like it can swallow you whole if you're not careful. But here—" I gestured at the steady waves hitting the rocks below, "it feels tamed somehow. Busy, restless, like it has to keep up with the city. Almost like it's carrying everyone's secrets."

She rested her chin on her knees, staring out at the darkening horizon. "Maybe that's why people keep coming here. To let the sea hold their secrets for a while."

I looked at her profile against the orange sky, her hair flying around her face. She seemed lost in thought, but all I could feel was the silence pressing in on me. The kind that made me both content and uneasy at once. I reached for her hand, and she gave it without looking, her fingers warm against mine.

Days past more rapidly and I was still a lot behind. It was a quiet Sunday afternoon. We curled up on the couch beside me while I scribbled notes for my exams. The television played in the background, muted, filling the silence with moving images.

Her phone lit up on the table. I glanced at the name flashing on the screen but said nothing. She looked at it too, her lips tightening, and let it ring out.

A few minutes later, it buzzed again. The same name. This time she picked it up.

"Hello?" Her voice was cautious, low. She listened in silence, her expression started shifting. First confusion, then disbelief, then something heavier started settling in. She turned away from me as if to shield her face, but I caught the faint tremble in her shoulders.

When she finally cut the call, she stood frozen for a moment, the phone still in her hand. Then she turned toward me, eyes already glistening.

"What happened?" I asked, my chest tightening.

Her voice cracked as she spoke. "It's Mom… she's in the hospital."

The words hit like a blow. She tried to steady herself but the tears came anyway, rolling down her cheeks. I rushed to her, pulling her into my arms, her body trembling against mine.

She buried her face into my chest, her sobs muffled. I held her tighter, whispering things I wasn't sure I believed—*She'll be fine. Everything will be okay.*

She shook her head, tears falling fast. "I want to go home, Adi. I can't just sit here when she's lying there"

"We'll go if we have to. But right now, let's wait for another call. Maybe it's not as bad as it sounds." My voice was steady, but inside I felt the same helplessness clawing at me.

She was getting impatient and there wasn't much that I could do. Hours later, her phone rang again. She grabbed it in an instant, answering with shaking hands.

"Hello?!"

A pause. Then her face softened with disbelief. "Mom?"

Her mother's weak but reassuring voice came through the speaker. "Yes, it's me. I'm okay, beta. The doctors say it was just age… and stress. Nothing to worry about."

Tears welled again, but this time they carried relief instead of fear. She pressed the phone tighter to her ear, closing her eyes. "Don't scare me like that again, please."

When she hung up, she collapsed against me, utterly drained. "She's fine," she whispered, more to herself than to me.

After few moments, she was still trembling, and looked at me with red, swollen eyes.

"I want to go home, Adi. I need to see her with my own eyes."

"Then I'll come with you," I said immediately. The decision felt like instinct, as if there was no other option.

But she shook her head, firm. "No. Your exams are in just a few days. You can't miss them because of me."

I reached for her hand. "Radhika, don't be ridiculous. How do you expect me to sit here with books when you're going through this? I'll manage my exams.."

"No, Adi," she cut me off, her voice steady despite the tears. "This is not negotiable. You can't throw away something so important. I'll go. You'll stay. That's final."

I wanted to argue more, but the determination in her eyes stopped me. For the first time, I realized she wasn't asking me.

The next morning, silence lingered between us as we packed her bag. When we reached her apartment, she immediately called her office to ask for leave. I sat on the couch, pretending to read a message on my phone, but my eyes kept straying to her. She was there in the same room, yet I could feel her slipping away, pulled by duties and distances I couldn't bridge.

When she hung up the phone and turned toward me, she smiled faintly. "It's done. They've approved my leave."

I forced a smile back, but inside, the weight pressed harder. She was choosing responsibility, and I was left my fears.

We took a cab to the Bus station. She stood before me, ticket in one hand, her other hand trembling against mine. I carried her heavier bag, reluctant to let go even of that small burden. When the conductor called, she looked up with a practiced smile that barely reached her eyes. "It's just a few days, Adi. Focus on your exams. I'll be back before you know it."

I didn't answer, only pulled her into me. The hug stretched on too long, too tight, as though both of us feared what would come once we let go. Her head rested against my chest, and I wished I could freeze the moment and stop the world from tugging her away.

"Take care of yourself," she whispered, voice trembling.

"You too," I breathed, though my heart screamed, don't leave me now.

Her eyes searched mine, shining with something unsaid. "Promise me you won't skip your exams."

I forced a smile. "Promise."

She let go first, her fingers slipping from mine like sand through an open hand. Then she turned, boarded, and found her seat by the window.

The bus groaned alive. She waved softly, and I raised my hand, though already she seemed farther away than the distance allowed. Slowly, the dust swallowed her face, her shape dissolving into the crowd until only absence remained.

And as I stood there, a weight pressed deep into me an unshakable knowing. That this wasn't just another goodbye. This was the beginning of an unraveling I wasn't ready for.

I walked back from the bus station with my mind still hovering around her. The city noises dull against the storm inside me. Every step felt heavier, as though I had left more than just her at the station. Something inside me had been torn away, and the hollow it left behind gnawed deeper with each breath. Home no longer felt like home if she wasn't somewhere in it.

I told her I'd focus on exams, but how was I supposed to line up words in my head when the only image burning in me was her, pressed against me in that last hug? Her fingers slipping away. That half-smile trying to be brave. The soft wave through the bus window.

That night, my phone buzzed and her name lit up the screen. I felt a sense of relief before picking it up.

"I've reached," she said softly, her voice carrying both relief and exhaustion.

'Good. How's Mom?' I asked.

"Mom's resting now. The doctor says she needs some more checkups in the next few days, but… it's nothing we can't handle."

"Alright, that's good to hear" I whispered. "Just promise me you'll take care of yourself too."

"I will," she said. "Goodnight."

The next few days moved in slow motion. I tried to force myself into my books. The rhythm of our calls began to falter, too. From long, late-night conversations filled with laughter and soft silences, they shrank to short updates, clipped words exchanged between her errands and my attempts at study.

Sometimes, I stared at my phone longer than the pages of my notes, waiting for her name to appear. When it didn't, I convinced myself she must be busy, or asleep, or with her mother. Still, the quiet between us felt louder than anything.

The night before my first paper, I sat on the couch staring blankly at the neatly stacked notes in front of me. My mind should have been on exams, but instead it was circling back to her, as it always did.

Just then, my phone buzzed. Her name.

I picked it up immediately.

"How are you, scholar," she teased gently, trying to sound cheerful. "Big day tomorrow?"

"Yeah," I said, rubbing my temples. "Feels like my brain is leaking already."

"You'll do fine, Adi. I know you." A pause, softer now. "I just wanted to wish you good luck."

Her voice steadied me more than any revision could.

"Thanks," I whispered. "That means more than you know."

After a pause, her voice softened, carrying a weight I hadn't heard before. "I took Mom for her follow-up checkup yesterday."

I sat up straighter. "And?"

"The doctor said… she shouldn't be left alone much now. Stress and age are catching up with her. She needs constant rest and someone around to keep her calm. You don't know how stubborn she can be," she said with a weak laugh, but I could hear the worry underneath.

I closed my eyes, imagining her mother lying on the bed, fragile, the house quieter than it should be. "That sounds serious," I said, the words dry in my throat.

"Yeah," she whispered. "I don't know how long she can manage like this without someone at home. I…" she trailed off, as if the thought was too heavy to put into words yet.

"Radhika," I said softly, not pressing her but feeling the unspoken tug in her silence.

She exhaled. "Anyway, Rohan came with his car. It was easier to take her that way."

The name cut through me, but I didn't react. Not now. Instead, I latched onto what mattered most. "You must be exhausted."

"I'll manage," she said, though her voice betrayed the cracks. "Adi, don't worry about us. You have your exams. Just focus, okay.

"Take care of her. And take care of yourself."

"I will," she replied, but there was a fragility in her voice I couldn't shake.

When the call ended, the exams in front of me felt trivial, almost cruel. All I could see was her face, torn between duty and desire, and a future I wasn't sure we had the strength to hold onto.

The days of my exams passed in a haze. I sat in those classrooms with answer sheets in front of me, but my mind rarely stayed tethered to the ink and paper.

By the time the last paper ended, relief didn't come. Just an empty weight pressing down on me. That evening, when my phone lit up with her name, I answered in the first ring.

"So" she teased softly, "how does it feel?"

I sighed, leaning against the wall of my room. "Feels… nothing, honestly. Just glad it's over. What about you? How's Mom?"

"She's better," she replied, though her tone carried a weariness no doctor's report could cure. "I'm making sure she eats and rests on time. It's… manageable. For now."

I hesitated, then said, "I think I'll go back to Nashik for a while. Mom's been asking, and with exams over, there's no point staying here."

She was quiet for a beat. "That's good, Adi. It'll be nice for you to be around friends and family. And honestly… I might take a while before I can return to Mumbai. Things here aren't steady yet."

Something inside me sank, though I tried to keep my voice even. "Yeah. Of course. Your mom needs you."

"She does," she whispered, and though her words were steady, I could sense the distance stretching between us—slow, quiet, but real.

We stayed on the phone until her voice grew heavy with sleep. When she finally whispered a soft goodnight, I laid staring at the ceiling long after, restless. Somewhere in that quiet, I knew going back home was the only thing left for me to do.

CHAPTER 13
LOVE QUARANTINED

THE NEXT MORNING, I packed a single bag. The apartment felt hollow, as though her absence had drained it of its warmth. I locked the door, lingered for a second in the corridor, and then walked away.

When the train rolled into Nashik, I spotted Karan waiting near the exit, leaning casually against his bike, waving like he had been there for hours.

"Finally," he said, clapping my back as I stepped out. "Back from the battlefield."

I managed a smile, though it didn't quite reach my eyes. "Felt more like thousand battles at once."

"Good," he grinned. "That means you need beer. And sleep. Not necessarily in that order."

We strolled past the auto's, and as he sped through the familiar streets of Nashik, I felt a strange comfort in the chaos. Yet beneath that layer of familiarity, my thoughts kept trailing back to her—to a house far away, where she sat beside her mother, carrying a weight I couldn't lift for her.

Karan dropped me off at home. I called her the moment I stepped into the house, but she didn't answer. Instead, I left her a message: *I've reached home.*

Home itself felt strange. Familiar walls, familiar smells, yet I couldn't settle into them. It was as if my heart had been left behind somewhere else.

Later, Karan showed up again like he always did in moments I couldn't carry myself. He pulled me out for a couple of beers at a dimly lit bar. He didn't waste time pretending.

"You look the same as you did after your accident," he said, eyes searching mine.

I forced a smile, shrugged. "It's nothing."

But we both knew he didn't believe me.

At dinner, Mom kept watching me, sensing something she couldn't put into words. Dad asked why I was pushing food around my plate instead of eating properly. I gave them vague answers, nothing that would betray the storm in my chest. Later that night, when the house was quiet and my thoughts were loud, she finally called. Her voice was soft, almost whispering so as not to wake her mother.

"Sorry… I couldn't pick up earlier. I was busy with housework."

I laughed it off, told her it was fine. Just hearing her was enough.

There was a pause, the kind that carries truth heavier than words. "I missed you," I said.

"I missed you too," she whispered back.

For a brief moment, the distance between us shrank, carried away by the honesty in her tone. I told her I would come visit in a few days, once I had spent some time with family.

She hesitated, then said, "That would be great if you came… but it's not necessary. I don't want you to trouble yourself."

Long after the call ended, I laid staring at the ceiling fan spinning endlessly above me. Every thought circled back to her. Her tired voice, her hesitation, her mother's frail health. I told myself I should just go, take the first train, stand at her doorstep, no matter what she said. She needed me, I needed her.

But before I could even shape those thoughts into plans, the world itself shifted.

News broke like wildfire. Rising cases, overflowing hospitals, masks and sanitizers vanishing from shelves. Every conversation at home was about infection counts, city after city shutting down, whispers of a lockdown looming over us like a dark cloud. Within days, it wasn't just whispers, it was reality. Streets emptied, shops closed, and every familiar rhythm of life was silenced. The World got infected with the Corona Virus.

I remember standing near the colony exit, looking out at the city's usually busy streets. They were deserted now, eerily quiet except for the occasional wail of an ambulance slicing through the stillness. The air itself felt heavier, thick with fear. My phone buzzed constantly with news updates and family. WhatsApp forwards images of crowded hospitals, doctors in suits that made them look more like astronauts than healers, desperate pleas for oxygen cylinders.

And there I was, trapped.

The world had shut its doors just when all I wanted was to run through one, to reach her. Bus stations closed, trains cancelled, borders sealed. Even stepping outside the house was suddenly a privilege wrapped in fear.

The distance between Nashik and Goa had never felt so insurmountable. Calls became our lifeline. Her mother needed care, she had her hands full with household work, and I could hear the exhaustion in her voice. I wanted to be by her side more than ever, but now the decision wasn't hers or mine. It was the world's.

It felt as though the universe had conspired to test us, locking us apart and pressing weight on the fragile threads of our bond. Love was supposed to pull people closer, but what happens when closeness itself becomes forbidden?

The days blurred into each other, marked not by dates on the calendar but by numbers on the news. New cases, new deaths, new rules. The world was shrinking inside four walls, and so was I.

With every call, I felt her slipping further. She wasn't mine entirely anymore. I tried to remind myself that love meant patience, that real love endured, but the ache was still there. Quiet, constant, corrosive.

Then, one evening, her voice carried a strange hesitation.

"Today I had to take Mom for her follow-up. It was impossible with just me, and the transport from here to city aren't running properly… so I called Rohan.

Her words felt like a stone dropped into my chest.

I wanted to ask a hundred questions—Why him? Why not someone else? But all I managed was, "Oh. Okay. If he helped, then… good."

"Adi… don't get upset, okay?"

She must have sensed the weight in my tone because she rushed to explain.

"Adi, please. Don't think too much. It was just for Mom. You know how things are here. I didn't want to worry you."

I said nothing. Silence thickened between us until she finally whispered,

"Say something."

"I just… I wish I could have been there," I muttered. "For you."

"I know you do."

"Just take of yourself and Mom. I will be there for you as soon as the world allows me."

"I hope the world heals soon." She said, almost praying.

"I do too."

That night, for the first time, sleep didn't just evade me, it mocked me. Every time I closed my eyes, I saw her standing beside him, grateful for his help. I knew it wasn't betrayal. I knew she loved me. But love wasn't always about what was true, it was about what the mind chose to believe in the quietest hours of the night.

And one day, patience gave up. The words I had swallowed for weeks finally clawed their way out.

We were talking about the chaos around us when she mentioned Rohan again. His name was no longer rare. It was threaded through every conversation. He helped her take her mother to the hospital. He brought groceries during the lockdown. He even fixed something at their home.

Before I knew it, my voice was sharper than I intended.

"Maybe that's the reason you don't pick up my calls anymore."

Her silence stung before she spoke, low, almost pleading.

"Don't say that, Adi."

"Why not? Rohan and you, suddenly he's everywhere. And you keep telling me, like it's natural. Do you even realize how it makes me feel?"

"He's just being helpful. We've known each other since we were kids. That's all."

"Oh, so now you're defending him." My breath came hard, uneven. "Do you understand what it looks like from here? He's always around you. You mention him in every other sentence. Don't I understand where this is going?"

Her voice broke as she tried to explain.

"It's not like that. Adi… do you want me to lie to you instead?"

"No. I want—" My throat locked. Words burned inside me. I want you only to need me. *I want to be the one beside you, not him.* But what came out was ragged, incomplete.

"I want you… I…"

She cut me gently, her tone breaking into tears.

"Please stop. You know I'm all alone here. At least he's here helping me. Do you think I want this? Do you think it's easy for me?"

Her words should have comforted me, but instead they tore deeper.

"What's that supposed to mean? Do you think I wouldn't be there if I could? If it wasn't for these walls, these rules, this damned lockdown—don't you think I'd already be there?"

"I didn't mean it that way," she whispered. I could hear her crying now.

Something inside me crumbled. The anger drained, leaving only shame and longing.

"I'm sorry," I said softly. "I shouldn't have snapped. I just… I hate this distance. I hate that I can't be the one standing next to you. I know how this makes me feel. But maybe I don't always know how it makes you feel."

Silence stretched between us, heavy but alive. For the first time, it felt like we were both breaking, not just apart from each other, but inside ourselves. The night after our fight stretched endlessly. I heard her voice—tired, trembling, edged with tears. I kept replaying my own words, the sharpness of them, and hated myself for it.

The next morning, I stared at my phone for hours, willing it to ring. It didn't.

I typed a message, erased it. Typed again, erased again. Nothing felt enough. Nothing felt right.

By evening, she finally called. Her voice was steady, almost too steady.

"Adi, let's not fight again, okay?"

It wasn't a plea—it was a boundary.

"I don't want to fight either," I said quickly. "I just… I miss you. That's all it is."

"I know." Her sigh carried more weight than words. "But things are already hard enough here and I can't afford to waste energy on arguments. I need peace, Adi. Please."

Her words weren't cruel, but they cut anyway. Peace. I wanted to be her peace, but instead, I was turning into another storm.

"I'll try," I whispered.

"You don't have to try," she said. "Just… trust me."

Trust. The word lingered long after the call ended. I wanted to believe it was that simple. That if I held on long enough, things would fall back into place.

But as the days rolled on, I felt the invisible gap widening. Her calls became even shorter, her laughter rarer, and though she never said it outright, I could sense she was holding parts of her life away from me. Whether to protect me, or to protect herself, I couldn't tell.

Even though we didn't fight, the signs of fading affection were everywhere. The words that once came rushing now arrived reluctantly, almost forced. "I love you" became rare, and when it did pass between us, it sounded more like a ritual than a confession. A custom we both kept alive so the silence wouldn't swallow us whole.

She no longer mentioned Rohan, but she didn't need to. His absence in her words only confirmed his presence. Yet deep inside, I knew he wasn't the only problem. He was just a shadow in the corner of the room.

The real enemy was time — relentless, cruel, always playing with my fate. Time that stretched the distance between us, time that tested patience, time that turned our promises into echoes. What once felt eternal now felt fragile, as though every passing day stole another thread from the fabric we had woven together.

I told myself love was stronger than circumstance. But when even love begins to sound like duty, you can't help but wonder — are we holding on to each other, or are we only holding on to what once was?

After a few days, our conversation drifted, as it always did, to the rising numbers in Mumbai. The suffocating hospitals, the sirens, the stories of people who didn't make it. Somewhere in between, we admitted we were grateful, in a strange way, to have left the city before the lockdown sealed us in.

It was then she said it, softly, almost as if she wished the words could dissolve before reaching me.

"Adi… I've quit my job. I won't be coming back."

Her tone carried an apology she didn't speak, and though I had long known this day would come, the words still cut through me like a dagger.

"You're doing the right thing," I managed, my voice steady but hollow. What I wanted was to tell her to reconsider, to fight for the life we had built there. Instead, I betrayed myself with quiet acceptance.

"I'll look for something here, when the pandemic ends," she added, almost as if offering a bandage for a wound too deep.

"Hmm," I murmured, my throat dry, unable to summon anything else.

She knew exactly what was churning inside me, but chose silence. And so I broke it.

"Where does that leave us, Radhika?" I asked, the question carrying more weight than I could bear, hoping for an answer, a solution, a promise.

Her pause was long enough to make my heart sink.

"Honestly… I don't know, Adi. I just want the world to get back to normal."

But she didn't know what I already did. My world had a name, and it was her.

The days after her decision felt heavier. Something in me had shut down. My words were shorter. My laughter forced. I thought I was hiding it, but she noticed.

One evening, her voice cut through the small talk.

"Adi… what's wrong with you?"

I forced a chuckle. "I'm fine. Just tired."

"No," she said firmly. "This isn't just tiredness. You barely say anything now. And when you do, it feels like you're holding something back. Did I do something? I've been noticing it. You don't speak the same way anymore. You don't call me first. And when we talk, it's like you're trying to make me feel guilty. What's going on?"

Her directness cornered me. I wanted to say nothing, to let it slide — but the dam cracked.

"I *did* call you," I said sharply. "But you hardly ever pick up the first time. You're always busy with something else. It feels like… you don't need me anymore. The world isn't the same, Radhika. How do you expect me to remain the same in all this?"

"That's not fair. Do you even realize what my days look like? Running around all day, praying every night that she doesn't catch the virus. And now you're saying I don't need you? Adi, I'm fighting just to hold life together here. I'm drowning here."

"And while you're drowning, where does that leave me?" I burst out. "Always hearing about Rohan helping you, always being reminded that I can't be there. Do you know what that does to me?"

Her tone hardened. "Stop dragging Rohan into this! He helps because he's here. Because I don't have anyone else around me. If that makes you insecure, maybe the problem isn't him—it's you."

Her words cut deep, but I forced mine out, raw. "I am trying to save us, Radhika. Always thinking about what I can do to make things better for you. I am constantly imagining a future where we are still together, where we take care of our parents, where none of this distance matters."

Her reply came like a blade, trembling but merciless:

"How can you talk about taking care of me and my mom when you haven't even created a future for yourself?"

The world stopped. Her words shattered me in a way nothing else ever had.

Almost instantly, her voice faltered. "Adi… I didn't mean it. Please, I—"

But it was too late. The silence that followed was heavier than any fight we'd ever had. The call ended on an abrupt note. No goodnight. No I love you. Just silence, then the hollow click of disconnection.

Her words kept circling in my head like a curse: *"How can you talk about taking care of me and my mom when you haven't even created a future for yourself?"*

I stared at the phone screen long after it went dark. A dozen times it buzzed with her name flashing across it. I couldn't bring myself to answer. Not out of pride, not even out of anger anymore, but because I didn't know what I would say if I did.

The silence grew louder than her voice ever had.

Lying on my bed, I felt every failure pressing down on me. I hadn't made the career I once dreamed of. I was still scrambling, trying to prove myself in a world that had stopped moving. And she, she had seen it, pointed it out, thrown it at me like a truth I'd been running from.

Maybe she was right. Maybe I hadn't created a future yet. Maybe I wasn't enough.

The more I thought, the more the shadows inside me stretched. Anger at myself bled into anger at her. Anger that she couldn't see how much I loved her, how hard I was trying, how much I wanted to be her strength. Instead, she turned to someone else when she needed help.

Each time her call flashed, I let it ring out. Then I put my phone face down, as if hiding from her would quiet the storm in me.

But it didn't. The storm only grew.

Two days passed in a blur of silence. Each time I picked up my phone, I stopped myself from calling. Pride, anger, guilt—they all pulled me in different directions. But eventually, love outweighed everything else. I couldn't bear the emptiness any longer.

That evening, with trembling fingers, I dialed her number.

The ring barely lasted before someone picked up. Relief flooded me until I heard a different voice.

"Hello?"

It was her mother.

I froze for a second, then forced a smile into my tone.

"Namaste, Aunty. How are you?"

There was a pause. Then, her voice, fragile and tired:

"I am fine, beta… but Radhika isn't."

The world tilted. "W-what happened?" My throat tightened.

Her mother sighed, the sound heavy, like it carried years of fear in a single breath.

"She collapsed yesterday. A seizure. We rushed her to the hospital… the doctors have kept her admitted. She's stable now." Her voice cracked. "But they said… this should not be happening at her age. Her body is not coping with the stress. She keeps everything inside, Adi. She never tells me, never tells anyone…"

Each word was a knife, carving into me. I gripped the phone tighter.

"How is she now? Can I—can I talk to her?"

"No, beta. She's resting. The medicines keep her drowsy." Her mother's voice faltered again. "I am sitting outside her room and praying she wakes up smiling. But, Adi… I am worried. I have never seen my daughter this weak, this… broken. I don't know what's happening inside her heart, but it is hurting her body now."

Her words left me speechless. Shame and fear surged together, choking me. I had wanted to patch things up, to tell Radhika I was sorry. But I was already too late. The damage had gone deeper than I imagined.

Her mother's words echoed in my head long after the call ended. The voice played on repeat, each time stabbing me deeper. I couldn't sit still. I paced my room like a caged animal, fists clenching, unclenching, nails digging into my palms.

What have I done?

The fight, the silence, the accusations I had thrown everything at her, and she had been carrying her own storms all along. I thought I was the one hurting. I thought my insecurities were justified. But now, lying in some hospital bed, it was her who had paid the price for both our battles.

My mind spun with guilt.

If only I had picked up when she called back… if only I had swallowed my pride sooner… if only I had been strong enough to not make her feel more burdened than she already was.

Every "if only" became a blade. I wanted to run, to take the first train, bus, anything that could bring me to her side. To hold her hand, to tell her I was there, that I wasn't letting go. But the world outside my window was barricaded, guarded by silence and sirens. Lockdown had reduced me to a prisoner, watching the person I loved most fight her battles without me.

She needed me. And where was I? Sitting miles away, drowning in self-pity, while someone else—

My chest tightened at the thought. I didn't even have to say his name. I knew who must be there, filling the spaces I couldn't reach.

The very thought burned. He would be the one driving her to the hospital, talking to the doctors, fetching medicines. He would be the one her mother saw, standing steady when I was nothing but a trembling voice on the phone.

And me? What was I to her now? A burden? A man of promises with no proof?

I pressed my palms to my eyes, trying to hold back tears, but they came anyway, hot and relentless.

I am trying to save us, I had told her. *Always thinking about the future, about how we'll take care of our parents together.*

And she had said the words that still rang like a curse. Maybe she was right. Maybe I had nothing real to give. Just dreams. Just words.

But no matter how much I tried to reason with myself, one truth drowned everything else. She was my world. And my world was slipping away.

That next morning, I called her but it wasn't her voice I heard.

"Hello?" Her mother's voice came through, soft but edged with exhaustion.

"Aunty… it's me. Aditya."

There was a pause, then a sigh. "She's fine now. But she's sleeping."

Relief washed over me, only to be replaced by dread as her mother continued.

"I don't know what's going on in her mind, son. She doesn't tell me everything. But I can see the toll this is taking on her. And Aditya… I don't want my child breaking like this."

My grip tightened on the phone. Words stumbled inside me, but I couldn't push them out.

Her voice softened, carrying a weight heavier than any scolding.

"I want my daughter to be safe. To be happy. That's all I want. I hope you understand what I'm saying. I won't be with her forever, but while I am here, I want to see her settled. Only then will I have peace in my heart."

The silence after her words was crushing. It felt like she wasn't just speaking as a mother, but as fate itself reminding me of everything I hadn't built yet, everything I couldn't promise.

I swallowed hard, forcing my voice to stay steady.

"I… I understand, aunty."

But the truth was, I didn't. Or maybe I did, and that was what scared me most. When the call ended, the room around me felt heavier, darker. Her mother's words kept echoing—s*afe, happy, settled*—each one like a stone pressing against my chest.

"I'm failing her," I whispered into the emptiness. My voice cracked. "I'm failing everyone."

I thought of her lying in that hospital bed, fragile. A situation she didn't deserve. I thought of her mother, her tired voice trembling with hope and fear. And then I thought of myself—what was I? A man with no job, no plan, no way to protect the woman I loved. A man who could only offer words through a broken phone line while someone else stood by her side in flesh and blood.

The guilt twisted deeper. I punched the pillow, once, twice, until my knuckles stung.

"Why can't I be better? Why can't I be enough?"

My chest heaved as if I had run miles, but all I had done was sit alone in that dark room, drowning in the truth I couldn't escape: I wanted to be her world, but I had given her nothing to hold on to.

The sobs tore out of me raw, uncontrollable. I curled into myself, exhausted by my own mind, and somewhere between guilt and fear, I begged silently into the darkness.

"Please… just let her be okay. I don't care what happens to me. Just let her be okay. Now and forever."

That night, my phone lit up with her name. For a moment, I just stared at the screen, my chest tight. Then I picked it up.

"Adi…" Her voice was softer than I'd ever heard it, fragile but steady enough to make me breathe again. "I'm fine now. Don't worry. The doctors said I'll be discharged tomorrow. I'll call you once I reach home."

Relief flooded me, but it was tangled with guilt that burned hotter than anything else. The words tumbled out of me before I could stop them.

"Radhika, I'm so sorry… so sorry. I should have been there for you. I should have—"

She cut me off gently, but firmly.

"Stop. Not now. We'll talk tomorrow."

Her tone carried no anger, no softness either—just a wall I couldn't climb.

"Radhika, please, just listen—"

"Tomorrow, Adi," she repeated, and the line went dead.

The silence after the call felt heavier than any fight we'd had. Guilt crushed me from every side. If I hadn't snapped. If I hadn't let my insecurities spill over. If I had been stronger, steadier, better… maybe she wouldn't have broken down like that.

I turned over, buried my face in the pillow, but the storm inside me didn't quiet. I replayed every moment between us—the sweetness of our first calls, our dates, her birthday, our first kiss, her laughter that once made my days bearable, the promises we whispered in the dark. And then the silence, the doubts, the fights, the way Rohan's name became a wall between us.

Morning felt like a punishment. My body was heavy, my eyes stung from the tears and the sleepless night. When her name finally flashed on the screen, I froze for a second, staring, afraid of what this call might mean.

I picked up quickly, voice trembling.

"Radhika…"

Her tone was faint, tired. "I'm home now."

Relief hit me so hard I had to sit down. "Thank God. Are you okay? Did the doctor say—"

"I'm fine," she cut me gently. "Weak… but better. Don't worry."

But I couldn't help it. Words spilled out, broken and desperate.

"I'm sorry, Radhi. I should've been there. I should never have let things get this bad. It's my fault. I—"

She stopped me mid-sentence, her voice firmer than I expected.

"Adi, not now. Please. I don't want to talk about it today."

The silence that followed was unbearable. My throat locked.

"But—"

"Tomorrow," she said softly. "We'll talk tomorrow. Right now, I just need to rest."

And before I could plead, explain, beg—she ended the call.

The line went dead, leaving me hanging in that hollow space.

The days that followed were torture.

She called, but only in fragments, small, practical sentences.

"I'm fine now."

"Don't worry, I took my medicines."

"I'll sleep early tonight."

No warmth. No laughter. No us.

And yet, I clung to those scraps like a man starving, apologizing every chance I got. "I'm sorry, Radhi… I should have been better. Please forgive me."

Her silence was answer enough.

Then, one evening, her call came. For the first time in days, there was no tiredness in her voice—only a quiet resolve that made me shiver. A part of me already knew this was going to happen. I just didn't want to believe it or except the truth. The truth of the fact that destiny had again defeated me.

"Adi," she said slowly, "I think… we should take a break."

The words punched the air out of me. And here I was lost again to hands to cruel hands of fate. As if the world got a kick out off making a fool out of me. Not once, not twice but whenever I loved something, it found a way to snatch it away from me.

The words punched the air out of me. "What? Radhika, no… don't say that. Please don't. I'll change, I'll fix everything, I—"

"Adi," she interrupted softly but firmly, "this is not about changing. Right now, I can't handle the stress of us… the fights, the distance. It's crushing me."

I couldn't breathe. My heart clawed for a way out, for some argument strong enough to hold her.

"No, Radhika. Don't do this. You're all I have. I'll wait through anything, I'll fight through anything, just don't say it's over."

"It's not over," she said, her voice breaking. "But right now, I need space. I need to breathe without guilt or fear. Please understand."

I felt tears rising, but I swallowed them back. I wanted to fight harder, to pull her close through the invisible walls between us, but one look at what had happened to her health was enough to chain me down.

"Okay," I whispered, broken. "If this is what you need, I won't stop you. But Radhika know this—I'll wait. No matter how long, no matter what happens. When the world heals, when you heal… I'll still be here. For us."

On the other end, there was only silence. Then a faint, muffled sob before the line went dead.

I sat there, phone pressed to my ear, listening to nothing but the echo of a promise I didn't know if I could ever keep. It wasn't just her words that broke me. It was the sob behind them, the unspoken truth that maybe she had already left me behind.

I wanted to throw the phone across the room, but instead I held it tighter, as if clutching it could somehow bring her back. My mind replayed her voice on loop, that soft finality in her tone. *"I need space. Please understand."*

Space.

That single word became a chasm, stretching wider and wider until it felt like it would swallow me whole. I truly feared not just losing her, but losing myself in the silence that would follow.

The days that followed were quieter than death. No calls, no long conversations that once stretched into the night, no laughter filling the silences. Just the emptiness of my phone screen staring back at me, reminding me of her absence.

I kept waiting for the ping of a message, for the vibration of an incoming call, for something that would tell me she still needed me. But hours bled into days, and the days dragged themselves into weeks. The silence stretched, heavy and unkind, until it became the only sound I knew.

The world outside, however, had begun to stir. Restrictions were being lifted slowly. Shops reopened, masked faces moved about, and news channels ran stories of "life returning to normal." But nothing felt normal to me. My world hadn't moved forward with the calendar, it had frozen in the moment she said break.

Two months. That's how long it had been since her words split my world apart. Two months of waiting, of checking my phone more than I breathed, of sinking further into myself.

With nothing to escape into, the days stretched endlessly—one bleeding into the other until I stopped knowing what day it was. College had not started again. And even if it did, I wasn't sure that I would be going back to Mumbai.

Mornings became afternoons, afternoons became nights, and I barely noticed. I'd wake up late, not because I was tired, but because there was no reason to wake up at all. The phone would be the first thing I checked, and when her name wasn't there, the heaviness of the day settled instantly. Sometimes I'd scroll through old chats, reread the "I love you" that once meant everything, and wonder how words so alive back then could now feel like fossils.

Some nights I thought about calling her, just to hear her breathe, but I never did. Fear stopped me. Fear that she wouldn't pick up. Fear that even if she did, the distance between us had already won.

And yet, every day, I told myself: *Tomorrow. Tomorrow she'll call and say she misses me. Tomorrow she'll tell me she's ready.* But tomorrow always came empty, carrying nothing but silence.

My parents noticed. My mother would leave breakfast on the table and sigh when she came back hours later to find it untouched. My father kept asking if I'd thought more seriously about finding something to do.

"Adi," he said gently but firmly, "you should start thinking about finding a job now. Your last year of college is going to continue with online lectures for a while, and sitting idle isn't helping anyone. It would be better not to lose more time."

I couldn't deny it. He was right.

Her voice flashed in my head, cruel but true: *"How can you talk about taking care of me and my mom when you haven't even created a future for yourself?"*

And if there was any chance, just any that she would come back, then I needed to be the man who had a future, not the boy who wasted his days mourning what he had lost.

Weeks passed, and I tried to keep my promise to myself. Slowly, painfully, I dragged my days into some sort of rhythm. Applications, emails, interviews. Most ending with silence or rejection. But one morning, after weeks of trying, I finally heard the words I had been waiting for.

"Congratulations, Aditya. Welcome aboard."

For a moment, I just sat there, numb. A job. My first step into the future. The one thing I had failed to create before. The very thing she had once used to break me down was finally mine. And in that instant, all I wanted was to tell her. To share the news, to hear her voice light up with pride, to feel that maybe this was proof I could be the man she had doubted I could become.

I unlocked my phone, scrolling to her name, my fingers trembling over the keyboard. But just as I was about to type, my screen buzzed. A notification.

It was her.

Not a message—no. A social media post.

I opened it, and the world stopped. But this time only for me.

There she was, smiling. Dressed in colors brighter than I remembered, her hand extended forward, a ring shining on her finger. Next to her, standing tall and proud, was Rohan. The caption was simple, almost cruel in its plainness:

"Forever begins here"

My breath left me in one sharp pull. My vision blurred. For one tiny moment in months, I had felt the warmth of hope. The fragile spark of moving forward. And in the very next, it was ripped away, crushed under the weight of a single photograph.

The job, the struggle, the tiny victory. It all felt like ash in my hands. Because in the end, what was the point of building a future, if the person you wanted to share it with had already chosen hers with someone else?

I dropped my phone onto the bed, my hands shaking, my chest burning. The room around me spun, but the only image that stayed still, sharp as a blade, was her smile—her smile, for someone else.

My mind refused to accept it. *No… this isn't real. It can't be. Maybe it's some family thing, maybe it's just a photoshoot… maybe—*

But the ring. That damned ring. It gleamed like proof carved out of my own nightmares. And Rohan—Rohan standing beside her, not me.

My chest tightened, my throat locked. A scream clawed its way up, but it came out as a broken gasp. I grabbed the phone again, staring at the photo till my eyes watered. The comments below blurred into nothing but noise: *Congratulations, perfect couple, made for each other, finally!*

Each word felt like another stab. Perfect couple? Made for each other? That was supposed to be us. That was supposed to be me.

Before I knew it, the phone slipped from my hand and hit the floor. I pressed both palms into my eyes, trying to shut it all out, but the images only grew clearer. Her laugh. Her promises. The way she once said *"Adi, you're my world."*

And now… she was someone else's.

I stumbled to my desk, the anger finally tearing through the grief. My fist slammed against the wooden surface, once, twice, until it hurt. The sting in my knuckles was almost a relief, at least it reminded me I was still alive, still capable of feeling something other than this hollowness.

"Why?" I shouted into the emptiness of my room. My voice cracked, echoing back at me like mockery. "Why do you always do this to me? Every time… every damn time I try to hold onto something good, you find a way to rip it away."

The walls didn't answer. The silence that followed was heavier than the scream itself. I sank to the floor, my back against the bed, my chest heaving. My inner voice was merciless.

You weren't enough. You never were. She wanted stability, a future, a man who could protect her. And you? You had nothing. No job, no success, no strength. Just empty words. He gave her everything you couldn't.

I covered my ears as if I could shut the thoughts out, but they only grew louder. Tears finally spilled, hot and uncontrollable, blurring everything around me.

"I was building this for us," I whispered, broken. "I wanted this… for us. For her. And now…"

The room swam before me. Hours passed, maybe, or just minutes, I couldn't tell. The only thing I knew for sure was that the tiny spark of hope I had carried through months of loneliness had been crushed under that one photograph.

My hand moved before my mind could stop it. I picked up the phone and dialed her number. Once. Twice. Thrice. She didn't answer. I refused to stop. My thumb kept pressing the green button, stubbornly, desperately, until finally the line clicked.

"Radhika…" my voice broke as her silence filled the gap between us.

What came after, I cannot bring myself to say. Some truths aren't meant to be repeated, even inside your own head. All I know is that by the time the call ended, I was hollowed out like she had ripped away the last piece of me that was still standing. Her voice kept replaying in my head, each word cutting deeper than the last.

I stared at the ceiling of my room, but the walls seemed to close in. My chest tightened until I couldn't take it anymore. The voices in my head got louder and relentless.

You've failed again. You couldn't keep her. You're a burden. You'll never be enough.

I wanted to shut them down. I wanted silence.

And I knew only one way.

I walked out, ignoring my parents' questions, ignoring the worried tone in my mother's voice. My bike carried me through the night until I stopped at a bar I had never stepped into before.

The first drink burned my throat, but it dulled the edges of my thoughts. The second blurred them. By the third, I wasn't Adi anymore. I was just a body trying to forget.

Glass after glass. Bottle after bottle. The noise around me didn't matter. The world didn't matter. Only the numbness did.

I didn't answer my phone. Didn't want to. My parents must have tried a hundred times. I didn't care. Eventually, they called Karan.

Karan told them I was with him. But he knew I wasn't. He searched.

It was past midnight when he found my bike parked outside the bar. He walked in and spotted me slouched at the counter, eyes bloodshot, my hand wrapped around another drink. My shirt was damp with spilled liquor. My head hung as if it weighed more than my body.

Karan froze for a second, like he couldn't believe it was me. Then he walked up, sat beside me, and ordered water. He didn't say anything at first. He just looked at me, his silence heavier than the music in the background.

"Adi," he finally said, softly, almost breaking. "What are you doing, man?"

I laughed, but it wasn't laughter, it was hollow, cracked. "What does it matter, Karan? She's gone. Everything's gone. Nothing left to save."

He clenched his jaw. I could see the pain in his eyes, like he wanted to shake me back into myself. Instead, he just put his arm around me.

"You're not gone," he said firmly. "Not while I'm here."

I shook my head, tried to lift the glass again, but he snatched it away and slammed it on the counter. "Enough!" he snapped, his voice cracking.

I wanted to fight him, argue, but the words wouldn't come. My body gave up before my mind did.

Without asking, Karan pulled me up. I stumbled, barely able to walk, but he held me—half dragging, half carrying me out into the cold night air.

He didn't take me home. He knew I couldn't face my parents like this. Instead, he took me to his place. He laid me on his couch, threw a blanket over me, and sat nearby, watching like I might disappear if he blinked.

This wasn't just heartbreak anymore. This was the start of my downfall. This was me giving up now. No more fight left.

CHAPTER 14
FINAL CONFRONTATION?

THE CLOUDS THICKENED, pressing in from every side, until all I could see was that lone figure tumbling below me. The air roared past my ears as I fought against it, desperate to close the distance.

"Hey! Hold on! I'll reach you—just don't give up!" I shouted, my voice raw, cracking.

The boy didn't answer. He kept falling, weightless, as if he had already surrendered to the void. I pushed harder, arms burning, lungs tearing, willing my body to move faster.

Closer. Just a little closer. And then, the haze shifted. The figure's face tilted upward, the light cutting through for the first time.

My breath locked in my throat.

My body froze mid-dive.

It wasn't a stranger.

It wasn't anyone else.

A fifteen-year-old boy, dressed in a white cricket uniform, bat slipping from his hands as he tumbled into the abyss. His eyes, wide and innocent, locked with mine, filled not with fear, but with a quiet acceptance, as though he already knew where he was going.

It was me.

I jolted awake, the dream still clinging to my skin like sweat. My chest heaved as I sat on the edge of the bed, trying to slow my breathing. I dressed quickly, knotting my tie with mechanical motions. As I stepped out, bike keys in hand, my phone buzzed. Karan's name flashed on the screen.

"Hello?" I said, adjusting the strap of my bag.

There was silence on the other end, only his unsteady breath. Finally, he spoke, two words that said everything:

"Bharat's father."

My grip on the phone tightened. My eyes shut instinctively, as if shutting them could block out the weight of those words. I didn't need more explanation. I knew.

"I'll meet you there," I whispered.

The hospital corridors were as suffocating as I remembered. Too white, too sterile, too full of grief. I found Karan by the entrance, his face grim, and together we made our way inside.

There, in the waiting hall, we saw Bharat. His shoulders hunched, his face buried in his hands. When he saw us, he staggered forward, and the next moment he collapsed into our arms. His sobs shook through us, raw and helpless.

We held him tightly, trying to keep him from breaking, but what comfort could we offer? Watching a friend shatter in front of you, it was like watching a mirror crack. Pain seeped into us all. We could see his world crumbling, but we couldn't stitch it back for him. You can only hold on, pray your grip is enough to keep them from shattering completely.

The day stretched into a blur of shadows and hushed voices. Relatives poured into the hospital, some wailing, some whispering. Bharat sat on the floor, head buried in his knees, while his mother stared blankly at nothing, her grief beyond tears.

By afternoon, we followed the ambulance carrying his father's body back home. The house, once alive with warmth, was now cloaked in silence broken only by cries of mourning. The smell of incense mingled with the heavy air of grief.

The final rituals had to be performed. The courtyard filled with people.

Neighbors, relatives, family friends, all gathered to pay their last respects.

I stood a little distance away, watching Bharat. His hands trembled as he lit the pyre. His mother's cries pierced the air, raw and uncontainable. Karan stood beside me, eyes lowered, silent.

I looked at Bharat, his face streaked with tears, his body rigid with the unbearable weight of responsibility. He had to stand strong for his mother, for the people around him, even as he was breaking inside.

A chill ran through me. And I was not ready to accept the reality that time will defeat me once again for sure. I can't defeat it, no one can. The flames crackled, sending sparks into the sky, disappearing into the wind. I swallowed hard, my chest heavy.

Inside, my thoughts screamed. Why does it feel like everything I love, everyone I care for, is always at the edge of slipping away?

When the rituals ended, Bharat collapsed again, and this time we didn't just hold him, we cried with him. Because in his loss, we felt our own. Watching Bharat stumble, barely able to stand, yet still carrying the weight of his family, I felt ashamed. Here was my friend, shattered, but still trying to hold the pieces together for his mother. And here I was, drowning myself in alcohol, letting my parents watch me slip away, giving nothing back to the people who still believed in me.

Few days later, Mom came into my room and quietly sat near my head. I tried to get up, but she stopped me, pulling my head gently onto her lap.

"Adi… don't you want to eat something?"

"No, Maa. I've already eaten outside," I mumbled, careful to keep my words slow, hoping she wouldn't catch the alcohol still lingering in my breath.

"You don't need to lie to me," she said softly. "And you don't need to hide your face. A mother knows everything… and a mother most certainly understands when something is hurting her child."

A single tear betrayed me, rolling down the side of my cheek. I wiped it quickly, not wanting her to see me weak.

"When you were born," she continued, her voice trembling but steady, "everybody was so happy. You completed our family. Not just me and your father—but the entire house, the relatives, everyone. You brought light with you. And when I see you now… cornered by life, struggling like this… it tears me apart."

"It's nothing, Maa. Just… work pressure," I lied again, my throat dry.

Her hand froze for a second. Then she asked quietly, "It's the girl you introduced us to at the wedding, isn't it?"

I couldn't bring myself to nod or deny. But the tears that broke free from my eyes said enough.

"You're my child," she whispered, stroking my hair, "and I know you loved her with every beat of your heart. But life hasn't been fair, Adi. It took her away. And still… I know my son. I know how I raised him. And I have not raised a boy who would throw his life away like this."

Her words shattered something inside me. The dam broke, and the tears came fast and heavy. I buried my face deeper in her lap, ashamed, broken, but comforted. Her saree grew damp under the weight of my grief, but she said nothing more. She just kept stroking my head, her silence stronger than any sermon.

I don't know how long she stayed like that. At some point, exhaustion finally dragged me under. For the first time in months, I slept soundly in my mother's lap.

That night something shifted inside me.

I didn't want to live like this anymore. Drowning in silence, alcohol, and unanswered questions. Either I would fight for her one last time, or… I would end it all. I didn't know which. Maybe both. But one thing was clear: I couldn't stay still anymore.

By morning, the decision had already grown roots in me. I would go to her. I would look her in the eyes, hear the truth from her own lips, and let that truth decide my fate.

A day later, I found myself sitting on a bus to Satara. My heart pounded with every turn of the wheels, not from excitement but from something darker, heavier. Goa still didn't have direct buses running as people weren't travelling much, not with COVID lurking everywhere, but that didn't matter.

I called Karan as soon as the bus left Nashik.

"I am leaving now."

"What do you mean you are leaving? To where?" he asked.

"To meet her."

"You're telling me you're on your way to Goa now? Where are you now?"

"In a bus."

"What! And you're telling me now? Get out of the bus right now. I will come with you as soon as I come back."

"What do you mean when you come back?" I asked.

"I'm in Mumbai. Visiting my sister. Mother wanted to meet her. We hadn't seen her for a long time. Enough about that. Don't act out of instinct. Let me come home first, then we'll talk."

"I'm sorry, I didn't know you weren't at home. I wouldn't have bothered you. But I have to do this alone."

"Don't be crazy. I'm not letting you go into an unknown territory all alone. I'm coming with you."

"Too late for that. And it's not an unknown territory. Someone I love… or at least someone I know stays there. Don't worry about me."

"Stop it, Adi. Which bus are you in?"

"Satara. A friend of mine from Mumbai stays there."

"Alright, stay with him until I reach there. I'll come by night and we'll go ahead." he replied.

"Karan… you're not going to do anything like that. You've already done a lot for me. I don't want to cause any more trouble to the people I care about. That's why I'm doing this alone."

"You are not alone. You never were. And I'm not asking. I'll be there as soon as possible. I'll find a bus or something. Stay there, and don't you dare turn off your phone. I will find you one way or another."

"Please don't."

Satara was halfway, and in Karad, just a little ahead, lived Shivam. He was one of the few real friends I had made during my time in Mumbai. Steady, grounded, the kind of guy who always carried care for others with him. I hadn't told him much about what had been going on in my life, but maybe I didn't need to.

All our memories, the time Radhika and I spent together, the moments we shared started coming back one after another. At first, it was the laughter, the silly arguments, the quiet evenings that made the world feel bearable. But then the unpleasant ones crept in. The fights, the silences, the harsh words we both wished we hadn't said. They were fewer in number, but sharper, and they started to replace the good ones, as if my mind was choosing pain over comfort.

I pressed my forehead against the cold glass of the bus window, hoping it would quiet the storm inside. Outside, the road stretched endlessly through fields I didn't recognize. The towns, the faces, all felt unfamiliar. I was in an unknown place. Not just outside, in this part of the world I had never seen before, but inside too. A place in myself I didn't know how to escape from.

Why was I going?

What did I hope to find at the end of this journey? Closure? Answers? Or a chance to rewrite what had already been written?

Maybe it was foolish. Maybe she had already chosen a life without me. Maybe by showing up, I would only wound myself further. But another voice whispered—what if? What if she was waiting for me to fight? What if she still cared, even a little, and just couldn't say it?

The bus rattled forward, the wheels humming a rhythm that felt like the pulse of my own thoughts—restless, relentless. Each passing mile only deepened the questions.

I shut my eyes and saw her smile, the one that used to melt away every storm inside me. But now it felt distant, flickering like a lone firefly in the dark. Stayed there for a heartbeat, then swallowed by the fog. I reached out in my mind, but she kept slipping away.

Was I chasing her? Was I going to reclaim my love, or bury myself in the ashes of it?

The bus rolled into Satara by late afternoon. As I stepped down, I saw Shivam waving, his smile wide as ever.

"Arre, Adi! Finally," he said, pulling me into a hug. We rode to Karad on his bike. Shivam's family welcomed me warmly. His mother insisted I eat first, his father asked about my journey as if I were one of them. For a fleeting while, the comfort of their household felt like a safe harbor, before the storm arrived.

As night fell, I kept checking my phone, waiting for Karan's call. Finally, a little after nine, Karan called.

"I will reach at the bus stop in ten minutes. Where are you?"

Shivam and I rushed to the bus stand. The dim yellow lights flickered above us, and the place felt eerily empty except for a few tea vendors and travelers waiting on broken benches.

The bus pulled in. Karan looked tired. His clothes wrinkled, a thin layer of dust on his face. But his eyes… his eyes were steady, carrying the same fire that had always pulled me back whenever I drifted too far.

He had traveled nonstop, from Mumbai to Pune, then another bus to Karad. The moment he saw me, he didn't speak. He just walked in and acted like everything was normal.

We had some refreshments there. Shivam looked at both of us, concern softening his face.

"Bhai, come back home with me. Have dinner, stay the night. You both look exhausted."

I smiled faintly, grateful for his warmth.

"Thank you, Bhai. Really. But we shouldn't. If we stay over, it'll only delay us. We'll take a room in a lodge nearby."

He nodded slowly, respecting my stubbornness. I hesitated for a moment, then glanced at him again.

"Actually… one more thing. Can I ask for a favor?"

"Of course," he said without blinking.

I took a deep breath. "Your bike. Just for tomorrow. I promise I'll return it by night."

For a second, I thought he might ask why, or where, or what for. But he didn't. Without a word, Shivam reached into his pocket, pulled out the keys, and pressed them into my palm.

"Take it," he said simply.

No questions. No conditions. Just trust.

This was the friendship boys shared. The kind where explanations weren't needed, where silence carried more weight than promises. I held the keys tightly, almost afraid I didn't deserve them.

"Thank you, Bhai," I said quietly.

He smiled. "Anything for my brother. Just ride carefully, and take care of yourself. Promise me one thing though, before you leave for Nashik, you have to sit down for dinner at my place."

I nodded, my throat heavy. "I promise."

We took a room near the bus stop. Nothing fancy, peeling paint on the walls, a single buzzing tube light, but it was enough for the night. The lodge had a small restaurant below, so we ordered some Chinese food to go along with the booze we'd picked up. Neither of us wanted to sleep on an empty stomach.

After a few drinks, Karan finally spoke. He didn't scold me, didn't lash out. He just leaned back with that crooked grin of his, the same one he always wore when he wanted to lighten the air.

"So… what did you tell at home? Where are you going?" he asked, twirling his glass in hand.

"Mumbai," I muttered. "For two days. Office work."

He raised an eyebrow. "Office work, huh? Hmmm. So… how's work?"

I couldn't help but let out a short laugh. He had me there. "You idiot," I said, shaking my head.

For a second, I almost apologized again for dragging him into this, for lying to my parents, for being the mess I was. But before I could say it, he changed the subject. Just like that. He knew better than anyone that some ghosts couldn't be chased with words.

A quiet settled between us. The food came, schezwan noodles, a plate of fried rice. We ate without much talk, the clink of spoons filling the silence. Somewhere deep inside, I wanted to call my mother, to hear her voice, but I didn't.

When the plates were empty and the bottles half-finished, we decided on tomorrow's plan. We'd leave before sunrise, ride straight through, and reach by midday. It was going to be a long ride.

Karan, drained from his endless journey, was asleep within minutes. I stayed awake, staring at the ceiling fan spinning above. My thoughts, restless as ever, carried me forward to the moment I'd see her again. Would I be able to hold myself? Would I even recognize the person she had become, the person who had left me behind?

I shut my eyes. Her face drifted in, soft at first, then sharper, almost cruel in its distance. At first, it was soft. She was laughing, the way she used to when I teased her about her handwriting. Her voice felt so close I could almost touch it.

But then the dream shifted. The air grew heavy, thick, and her laughter faded into silence.

"Adi…"

Her voice echoed, low and distant, as if it were slipping through cracks in a wall. My chest tightened. I knew this moment. My mind had buried it deep, but here it was—breaking free.

"Why are you calling me again and again?" she asked. The sharpness in her tone carried exhaustion, a finality I had never wanted to face.

"Because I needed to hear you," I whispered. But in the dream, my voice sounded like a scream. "Radhika, how could you do this? How could you—"

Her reply cut like broken glass.

"Don't make this harder, Adi. Please. What choice did I have? With the situation I was in, he was there—for me, for my mother. After I recovered, he asked her for permission to marry me. She said it was my choice. And I… I had no reason to deny him. He takes care of us. I've known him forever. It's over, Adi. I'm sorry."

"No… no, you can't say that." My throat burned, the words tumbling out jagged, frantic. "You're mine, Radhika. We fought, we broke, but we always found our way back. You can't just end it like this."

Her figure blurred in the dream, her face fading into fog, but her voice grew sharper, crueler in its truth.

"Adi, stop! I can't keep doing this. I chose peace. And it's not us anymore."

I reached out through the haze, desperate, clawing at shadows.

"Radhika, please! Don't leave me like this. Tell me it's not true. Tell me you don't love him."

For a moment there was silence. Then, her whisper, trembling yet firm enough to shatter me. Her face darkened, swallowed by shadow.

"I'm sorry, Adi. I don't love you anymore. I never loved you. He was my first love. He always will be."

The words slammed into me, louder than thunder. My chest seized, air ripped out of my lungs.

And then—silence. Her face dissolved, breaking apart into fragments of light that scattered into the void. I reached out, but my hands found only emptiness. The world beneath me gave way.

Suddenly, I was falling. The sky tore open, clouds swirling past in a blur. My body tumbled downward into the same endless white void I had seen before. But this time, I wasn't chasing anyone. I was the one plummeting.

Above me, faint and distant, I thought I saw her silhouette for a moment, her hand outstretched, then retreating. The harder I tried to reach, the farther she drifted, until she vanished completely.

Beside me, Karan stirred in his sleep, mumbling something before turning on his side. I stayed frozen, my fists gripping the blanket, as if the dream hadn't ended, as if I was still falling.

The morning air cut cold against my face as we rode out. Soon, we crossed a long bridge with a railway line glinting faintly below. For some reason, my stomach twisted. I kept my eyes on the road, but the faint sound of a train at the railway station just ahead lingered longer than it should have.

I shook it off, tightening my grip on the handles. The roads were still half-asleep, washed in pale light, the world yawning itself awake after a long, uncertain night. The wind roared in my ears like it was trying to silence my thoughts.

Karan sat behind me, quiet. The highway stretched endless ahead, fields glistening with dew, hills shadowed in morning mist. Every turn of the wheel brought me closer to her and yet, it felt like the distance inside me was only growing wider.

For hours, we rode in silence, stopping only for tea at a roadside stall. The newspaper pinned to the wall still screamed about the virus, about lives lost, about things broken. I sipped the steaming glass, my throat dry, my heart heavier than the road I had yet to cover.

Karan finally spoke, breaking the silence.

"So what's the plan? Are we abducting her? Is she getting married today? Are we planning to crash her wedding? Don't tell me we're abducting the bride. We should have brought a van."

Even in this situation, Karan managed to pull a laugh out of me, a sharp, unexpected sound that felt almost foreign in my throat. But behind the joke, his questions pressed against me like a weight I couldn't ignore.

What was I going to do?

Was I going to beg her to come back?

Or would I collapse in front of her, one last time?

I didn't know. I only knew that the next few hours held the answers I had both longed for and feared.

The road stretched endlessly, a ribbon of cracked tar cutting through fields that looked half-asleep under the sun. Sometimes we overtook trucks crawling with goods, sometimes buses with half their seats empty. Life was moving, yes. But slower, hesitant, like the world itself was unsure of what came next.

The wind slapped against my face, drying my eyes, yet no breeze was strong enough to clear the fog in my head. Every milestone we crossed seemed to pull me closer to an edge I couldn't see.

Karan hummed behind me, drumming his fingers on his knees as if trying to fill the silence I refused to break. But after a while, even he went quiet.

We stopped at a small dhaba by the highway. The cook stood idle, wiping already-clean plates. A lone bulb buzzed overhead though it was broad daylight. I barely tasted the paratha I forced down. Everything felt muted, as though life had turned its volume low.

Back on the road, I found myself glancing at every turn, every bend, as if half-expecting her to appear suddenly, waving me down, smiling like before. Foolish thoughts. But my mind wouldn't stop.

With every kilometer, the questions grew sharper.

Would she even agree to meet me?

Would she look through me like I was nothing more than a shadow from her past?

By the time we reached her town, the sun was on our heads. The houses grew closer, brighter in color, yet somehow quieter than the open highway we had left behind. Life here moved slower, untouched by the noise of the cities, but every passing face tightened the knot in my chest.

We slowed near the market—half-empty, half-alive. Shops shuttered, a few vendors selling vegetables behind makeshift masks, children darting between cycles and stray dogs. It should have felt ordinary, but for me, every corner whispered her name.

I gripped Karan's shoulder from the back seat. "Stop here," I said. My voice cracked, but he didn't question it. He pulled over near a tea stall, the bike's engine humming to a stillness that left the air too quiet.

For a moment, I couldn't breathe. My hands shook as I removed the helmet, the sweat on my forehead cold despite the heat.

Karan turned to me, his eyes steady. "So… this is it."

I nodded, though it felt more like I was collapsing inside than agreeing. My heart raced against my ribs, faster than it ever had on any cricket pitch, faster than any fight or exam or night of drinking could ever bring.

Beyond these narrow streets was her. The girl who had once been my firefly, who had lit up every dark corner of me and the same girl who had left me stumbling in the dark.

"I'll wait here. Call me if you need me." Karan said.

I reached her lane, the bike slowing under me until it finally stilled before the gate. For a long time, I just stood there, helmet in hand, staring. My chest rose and fell in uneven bursts. My palms were sweating, yet my whole body felt cold.

My breath came out harsh, uneven. The world around me blurred. Children's laughter from the far end of the lane, the clatter of utensils from some kitchen, a dog barking. All of it seemed too ordinary for the storm that was raging inside me.

This was the house where she lived. The same walls that sheltered her laughter, her tears, her silence. And now they stood between us, like a fortress I wasn't sure I had the right to enter anymore.

My hands gripped the iron gate. It rattled softly against its hinges, as if reminding me of the choice I had to make. To knock… or to walk away.

I could almost hear her voice in my head. Fragments of old conversations, the way she used to call my name when she was happy, the sharp edge in her tone the last time we spoke. The memories clashed until I didn't know which one was real anymore.

I swallowed hard. My chest felt tight, my knees weaker with every second I stood there. I wanted to scream, to beg, to collapse right there on the dusty road. But instead, I just closed my eyes.

And when I opened them, I forced my hand forward.

The gate creaked open. The sound seemed louder than it should have been, echoing in the quiet lane, scraping against my nerves. My hand trembled on the latch, my heartbeat thundering so hard I thought the whole street could hear it.

Inside, the path stretched toward the door, dim light spilling from a window, warm and familiar, too familiar. My throat clenched. I stood there, caught between the urge to run and the need to stay. Every second dragged, every breath heavier than the last. Somewhere in the distance, the train horn wailed, long and mournful, as if the world itself was warning me.

Finally, my legs moved. One step. Then another. The sound of gravel under my shoes filled the silence. My fists curled tighter with each step until I reached the door.

I raised my hand to knock.

And for a heartbeat, I hesitated, knowing that whatever happened beyond this door, there would be no going back…

The ride back was even more silent than the first one. But the silence was different now. It wasn't heavy with questions, it wasn't restless. It was the kind of silence that comes after a storm, when the air is still damp, the sky still carrying traces of thunder, but the worst has already passed.

Karan kept glancing at me whenever we stopped for tea or food, searching my face for answers I didn't offer. Sometimes he looked like he was about to ask, but the words never came. He understood in his own way that some truths didn't need to be dragged out, they lived in the quiet.

We switched places on the bike often, our bodies aching from the long road. By the time Karad's lights appeared in the distance, it was already far past sunset, the night folding itself around us.

At Shivam's place, the familiar warmth of his home wrapped around us like a blanket. We washed the dirt and dust from our skin, and for a while, over simple food and gentle laughter from his family, the weight of the journey loosened. It felt grounding, like stepping into a safe harbor after drifting too far at sea.

Shivam urged us to stay the night, but Karan had already checked the train schedule. There was one leaving past midnight. We thanked him for everything, for his bike, for his table, for his trust. Before leaving, I clasped his hand firmly.

"Come visit Nashik sometime," I said, my voice steady.

He smiled, nodding, as if he understood far more than I had spoken aloud.

We reached the railway station long before the train's arrival. The night air was still, broken only by the occasional honk of vehicles passing on the road above us. We sat on the overbridge we had crossed that morning, the faint glow of streetlights stretching shadows across the tracks below.

Karan sat beside me, silent for a while, his face heavy with questions. Finally, he spoke.

"So. Do you want to say something?"

I smiled faintly. "Yes. I do. Thank you for being there for me."

"C'mon. You know that's not what I'm asking. Did you meet her?"

I shifted my gaze from him to the endless sky. "No. I didn't."

He frowned. "You came this far, Adi. Didn't you want to at least speak to her, even once?"

"It's irrelevant what I might have said."

"You're making no sense now."

"I met her," I whispered. "But not the Radhika I fell in love with. She doesn't exist anymore."

Karan's eyes softened, and he understood without another word. Silence stretched between us, heavy yet strangely calming.

"I could see it in her eyes," I continued. "They still had their glow. But it wasn't mine to hold anymore."

"I'm sorry," Karan murmured. "But what about you? Will you be able to forget her?"

"Why would I want to forget her?" My voice cracked, but I forced it steady. "She was the best thing that ever happened to me. And now, she'll be my most treasured memory. She taught me how to live, how to dream again when my dreams failed, and how to fight my fears. Forgetting her would be unfair. She'll always be a part of me… like a light that showed me the way. My brightest firefly."

Karan's eyes brimmed with tears. "I'm proud of you, my brother. I'm sorry you didn't end up together."

"Yeah, I wished that too." I took a long breath. "But it doesn't take away what we had. I've always cursed time and fate for stealing what I loved the most. But now… now I'm grateful. For every single moment I had with her. My only regret is that I should have told her more often just how much I loved her." Tears blurred my vision, spilling freely.

"There's something special about our story," I said softly. "Even though we didn't end up together, it feels complete in its own way. I'll miss her, but whenever her name comes up in the future, I hope it brings me a smile—not pain."

"Wow," Karan whispered, his voice breaking.

I smiled through my tears.

"I need water," he said, standing up to buy a bottle from the shop at the end of the bridge. But as he turned away, I stopped him with words that had been circling my mind all night.

"You know," I said quietly, "there's something familiar about this bridge."

He looked back, puzzled. "What do you mean?"

I stared down at the tracks, the darkness yawning below us. "It's the same one from my dream."

And suddenly—I was there again.

The void stretched endlessly, white light spilling in every direction. No sky, no ground, just emptiness. I was standing still, yet my chest carried the weight of falling.

Then I saw him.

A figure stood in the distance, facing away from me. My steps echoed as I moved closer, each one heavier than the last. And when he finally turned… I saw me. Not the fifteen-year-old boy in cricket whites anymore. Not some younger shadow. He was me—here, now, with the same tired eyes, the same scars etched across his face.

"Why did you jump?" I asked, my voice trembling.

"I could ask you the same thing," the other me replied. His tone was calm, almost steady.

"Because you did," I shot back. "I was trying to save you. Why didn't you grab my hand?"

His gaze didn't waver. "And what do you think would've happened if I had?"

"I would have saved you."

"How?"

My mouth opened, but no words came. My chest tightened. "I would've… I…"

"That's right," he said softly. "You were falling too. There was no way you could have saved me. That's why I had to save you."

Anger pricked at me. "Save me? By jumping willingly? I saw you! You let go."

He tilted his head. "And what do you think was at the other end of that bridge?"

"I don't know," I muttered. "I only know I leapt after you."

"Yes," he said, voice gentler now. "But deep down… you know. You know what was waiting for you there. A world that doesn't belong to you anymore. If you'd kept running toward it, you'd have slammed into the dead end at full speed—leaving behind everyone who still loves you."

The truth cut deeper than any blade. My knees weakened as realization crashed in.

It wasn't me who had been trying to save him.

He was the one saving me.

"So, does my journey end here?" I whispered.

"That depends on you." He smiled faintly, almost kindly. "At least one road ends here. But when you open your eyes, you'll find yourself at a junction, with many roads leading ahead."

"So… what happens next?"

He shook his head. "I don't know. I haven't lived that part yet."

And just like that, the dream unraveled. The whiteness dissolved into sound. The rush of footsteps, the crackle of announcements, the screech of a train pulling into the station.

My eyes flew open. We had reached Kalyan. The train slowed beside us. We got off and sat on a bench for a while. We decided to wait for a while before taking the next ride home.

We reached Nashik in the evening. The house was silent when I stepped in. Only the faint hum of the ceiling fan filled the air. My father was sitting in the verandah, newspaper folded neatly on his lap, his glasses slipping slightly down his nose. He looked up at me, his eyes tired but steady.

"You're late," he said, not as a question, but as a simple fact.

I nodded and sat beside him. For a moment neither of us spoke.

"I'm sorry, Pappa."

He lowered the newspaper completely now, giving me his full attention.

"I'm sorry for everything," I said, my throat tight, words tumbling out before I could stop them. "I couldn't be the son you deserved. I've failed you again and again. You always stood by me, even when you didn't agree, even when I didn't deserve it. And still… I gave you nothing to be proud of. I just wanted to make you happy, Pappa. But I couldn't." My voice broke as the tears came. "I'm so sorry."

My father rose slowly, and for a moment I thought he might turn away. Instead, he placed both hands firmly on my shoulders, making me look into his eyes.

"Who told you I'm not proud of you?" he said, his tone steady, but there was a tremor beneath it. "Don't you ever think that. Listen to me—pride isn't about medals, or jobs, or success the way the world counts it. It's about who you are when life throws you down. And I have never seen a boy stronger than you. Every time you fell, you stood up again. Every time you were broken, you found a way to keep moving. That is pride, Adi. That is strength."

His eyes shone now, but he didn't let go. "You are a good man. A loyal friend. And the best son a father could ever hope for. I will always be proud of you. Always." His grip tightened. "Even when I am gone, I will still be here, right here." He pressed his hand to my chest. "So don't ever believe you are alone. I love you, my son. And I am proud, so proud to call you mine."

The dam inside me gave way. I broke down, collapsing into his arms. My body shook with sobs, my tears soaking his shirt, but he held me firm—steady, unyielding, the anchor I had by my side for all along. His embrace was not just comfort; it was a promise.

In his arms, I let everything go, the pain, the anger, the regret. And for the first time, I felt the faintest glimpse of peace.

I didn't know what waited for me beyond this moment, beyond this night. But as my father's hand rested on my back, grounding me, his words echoed in my mind like a prayer:

"Even when I am gone, I will still be with you."

I've been falling for as long as I can remember.

Not just in dreams… in life.

Since I was a child, I've always chased something—something I thought would make me whole. Sometimes it was a dream, sometimes a person, sometimes just the idea of happiness. I fought for them, clung to them, believed they'd save me. But one by one, they slipped through my hands.

There were promises I made, chances I missed, moments I let go of because I was afraid. I failed at things I wanted the most. I lost people I thought I couldn't live without. I even lost myself in the process.

There were days when I felt like all the bridges I crossed led only to the edge… and beyond that edge was emptiness.

But even after all that… I'm still standing. Because I learned that falling doesn't mean the end. It just means I have to find my feet again.

Yes, I've lost… I've failed… I've cried until I couldn't breathe. But that's not the whole story.

I still have my parents—those steady hands, those quiet smiles, that unconditional belief that I am enough. I still have friends, like Karan, Bharat and Nishant, who ask no questions, just stand by my side. I still have memories that make me smile through the pain, and scars that remind me I survived.

Life didn't give me everything I wanted. It didn't play fair. But it gave me something far greater, people who love me, who lift me when I fall, who believe in me even when I can't believe in myself.

So I choose to move forward. Not because the past wasn't painful… but because love, hope, and resilience are worth holding onto.

I may not know where this road leads. I may not have all the answers. But I know I'm not alone.

And that's enough to keep going.

So… what's of me?

I don't know yet.

I'd say the same thing the other me said…

I haven't lived that part yet…

flexibility is earned. If outcomes are missed, discipline is required. That's not indulgence. That's accountability in a modern form."

I looked across the stage. "And here's another truth. Balance cannot be imposed top-down. It has to be co-owned. Leaders must protect recovery time, yes. But Gen Z must also take responsibility for outcomes, not just hours. Balance works only when trust flows both ways."

The hall was quiet, pens scratching furiously across notebooks.

I looked around the hall. The faces told me everything—some carried the guilt of missed memories, others carried the fear of being judged lazy, and still others carried the exhaustion of trying to protect both clients and teams at once. Balance was no longer abstract. It was personal.

So we decided to close this session with simple, practical lessons. One for leaders. One for Gen Z. Both grounded in accountability.

For Leaders

- **Shift to outcome-based measurement.** Reward results, not late-night emails.
- **Design seasons, not marathons.** Allow intense sprints, but build in recovery after.
- **Protect boundaries visibly.** If leaders send emails at midnight, the culture follows. Model balance.
- **Respect life outside work.** People don't stop being human when they log off.

For Gen Z

- **Balance is earned through delivery.** Flexibility works only if outcomes are strong.
- **Set boundaries, but honour commitments.** Logging off is fair—but only after you've met your responsibilities.
- **Be transparent.** If you need balance, communicate it clearly instead of disappearing.
- **Respect shared sacrifice.** In crunch seasons, stretch with the team. Balance doesn't mean opting out of responsibility.

As the session drew to a close, I looked across the hall. The younger faces seemed relieved—validated that balance was not selfish but necessary. The older faces looked thoughtful, some still guarded, others softened by the stories they had heard.

We hadn't ended the tug-of-war. We had reframed it. Balance was no longer indulgence versus discipline. It was outcomes and seasons—stretch and recovery, effort and renewal.

CHAPTER SIX

THE PURPOSE PURSUIT